MURDER MAGIC AND MAYHEM

THE WITCH OF HENBANE ISLAND
BOOK 6

POPPY BRIDGEMAN

Ebook ISBN: 978-1-990509-70-4
Paperback ISBN: 978-1-990509-71-1
Audio book ISBN:978-1-990509-72-8

Cover created by Getcovers

FREE BOOK

Claim your copy of Magic Will Out when you sign up for my newsletter and follow Cossi as she seeks answers to her past.

1

I stared at the ceiling of my recently acquired home—the apartment over Raziel Books, also mine. One day ago, I'd accepted the role of protector without really knowing what it entailed. I'd been hoping for a long onboarding process from my mentor, Mrs. Vestum. I should stop hoping for things like a quiet life; it just gave the universe an easy way to turn my life upside down.

I didn't get even a day off between putting an end to a decades-long plot by my former mentor and getting the call to solve some problem on the mainland. In Vancouver, where people might recognize me as just plain old Cossi, and have no idea I was Cossi the protector of the magical world—one of them anyway.

I considered for just a moment running up to the solitary village and hiding in someone's back room. Azalea would let me. I could pour her drinks. But Jeffery wouldn't think twice about tracking me down and holding me to my responsibility—not only as a protector, but as a member of the council, and the committee struggling to find a way to counter all the threats to the magical world that came with selfies and social media posts.

And being the protector wasn't a 'maybe I'll do it' kind of thing. My power gave me three seconds to indulge my fantasy before it compelled me to head to Mrs. V's cottage for my marching orders.

Destroyer flew past me to wait on her doorstep as I approached it. "Think of all the crows I can recruit to my army. Possibly the first step to world domination!"

I looked at him as I opened the front door. "Hard to control an army you can't visit without my help." I spoke aloud, hoping Mrs. V would be able to give me advice on dealing with my familiar's megalomania.

"Details," he said in my head as he strutted ahead of me toward the kitchen.

"Tulip suggests he try it," Mrs. V said. Her lynx kitten familiar acted as a link between my crow and Mrs. V. I could hear them both, but I preferred not to listen to the bundle of menace. "She was laughing when she said it."

A cheerful laugh or a villainous muahahaha? "Good to know someone is able to resist his recruitment."

Tulip was in her bed cleaning her claws, like a gang boss loading his gun and staring at his victim. She was scary. She also looked like she'd doubled in size in the last couple of days.

"We're working on her social skills," Mrs. V said. "I told her I had no intention of living in the woods."

"What's the problem in Vancouver?" I asked, not ready to get into a discussion about lynx manners. "When do we leave?"

"I'm not coming," she said. "I think it would be helpful if you asked Didier or Mark to join you."

"But..."

She gave me one of her glares and I shut up.

"Trust your power, Cossi. Protector is a role you learn by doing. This incident is well within your abilities. And I have a phone."

Why did her compliment sound like a mild reprimand? Okay, maybe that was all me.

"So, what is this incident?" I might as well just go with it. She wouldn't put me into a position that could endanger the world—right?

"One of the children is leaking magic. The Vancouver council is worried about containing it. You will find they have very different views on protecting the community."

"Will they listen to me? I mean, this is my first job, and if they don't like my solution, how do I manage?"

She thought that one over. Her emotions were sliding out from under the shield she'd erected. Lilac for surprise, orange for worry, delicate blue for thought. Of course, I focused on the worry.

"I can see you fretting," Mrs. V said. "Your uncertainty is more likely to get in your way than the objections of the council. They cannot ignore you. They can act like children and try to obstruct you or convince you that their way is best. Do not let that undermine your confidence."

"You must act like you believe in yourself at all times," Destroyer said in my mind. "It embarrasses me as emperor of all animalkind to have a witch who looks weak."

All animalkind? "I will try my best."

"How urgent is this?" I asked aloud, ignoring the chatter between the two familiars.

"I suggest you leave today," she said. "I have few details, but this does need to be contained quickly—before the normal humans notice, or before the council does something we'll have to undo."

2

_____

I should just go home and pack. I mean, I didn't know if I could take spells or potions, or some other equipment. I'd look into getting a Protector Go Bag another time. But I would need clothes, and I needed to figure out how to avoid being recognized by people the old Cossi might know—a wig? A spell? But I still had questions.

"What do you mean we'll have to undo the council's work?" I asked. "Aren't there common rules?"

Mrs. V sighed at my lack of knowledge. How could she expect me to know anything since I'd only been on Henbane for less than three months, and didn't know I was a witch until I read the letter from my dad's lawyer?

"Should I stop asking questions?" I wouldn't, but it just bugged me that I was made to feel stupid for something I had no control over. And Destroyer said I should act like I was confident, right?

"No." She glanced at Tulip but didn't pass on the comment I overheard. The kitten actually took my side.

"I am not frustrated with you," Mrs. V said. "I'm frustrated with the situation and that we have no way of filling the gaps in your knowledge quickly. There are basic rules, but each community that exists among the plain humans will have their own adjustments. The rules of Henbane will not work anywhere that isn't isolated to witches and shifters."

I guess I understood. "Why wouldn't they have their own protector? I kind of know what they're facing because I lived as a plain human, but my parents took care of all the hiding business."

"There are only a few witches with the powers. It's not a job to be filled, it's a... I suppose the plain human term 'calling' fits. You will not be distracted by trivial concerns and politics. Your decisions cannot be anything other than protecting the world."

That was comforting and terrifying at the same time. It sounded like I couldn't do wrong, but if I had no understanding of the differences, how could I know that my powers were working on full information?

"You are not a puppet," Destroyer said. "The crow emperor would not be associated with you unless you were powerful."

"So do you know anything about the council members?" I wanted all the details Mrs. V had. "Have you met them?"

"Only on the phone," she said. "I no longer visit other communities. There are factions within the leaders. You will be tested, and must hold firm. I think we've all learned that people can seem open and friendly while harboring resentment and a willingness to kill."

That was one thing about the revelation that Phillip was behind the murders and had cast hexes to control the council that didn't make me feel naive. Everyone was fooled, even the woman sitting with me right now, the protector. Of course, that made me feel less competent.

"Go pack," Mrs. V said. "You have two choices to travel. We keep a vehicle in Sechelt which you can use. Then take the ferry. Or the shifters have a slot in a marina. You can ask Dolph to provide you with a boat."

"I don't know how to drive a boat," I said. But that's really what I preferred. Having my own transport would allow me to avoid ferry lineups and schedules.

"You will need to take someone," she said with a wave of dismissal. "You need to be in Vancouver today. You don't want the problem to get worse because you delayed."

Way to plant a seed of doubt. Oh, who am I kidding? That statement was a giant sequoia of doubt.

I called Dolph and he said a shifter would move Sea Wolf and drop off the keys in an hour. No argument, no list of warnings about damaging it, no question about who was driving it. Being the protector had some perks after all.

"Who should I take with me?" I asked Destroyer as I pulled out my overnight case. "I need someone who can take charge of the boat."

"You must take the opportunity to learn that skill," he said.

"Yes, the trip to Vancouver will provide time to learn," I said. "Who do you think will come?"

"The protector can take whoever she wants," he said.

"Fine. I don't want to order someone to join me. I'd like them to want to be there."

"You can make them want to," Destroyer said.

My protector power was the ability to make people do what I wanted. It came in handy getting a confession from Phillip, but I wasn't going to compel anyone. "I'll ask D and Mark," I said. There was no point in getting into a debate over free will with a megalomaniac crow.

"I advise you to take D," he said, completely confusing

me with his cooperation. "Mark is a cop. D is more flexible, and has powers that can help me with recruitment."

I'd warn D that Destroyer might ask for a snowfall or fog bank—I didn't imagine his plans included a sunny day. Not that my familiar could talk to D, but who knows what might slip out if I was tired enough.

D said he'd be over before the boat was ready. He wanted to tell his parents where he was going since they'd only just returned to Henbane.

I filled my case and took it down to the bookstore. Lance was looking up orders online and waved without looking up. I waited for him to finish.

"I'll be gone for a few days," I said, hoping I'd be back faster. The longer I stayed in the city, the more likely it was I'd run into a classmate and have an awkward conversation.

"Okay, you need me to look after anything while you're gone?"

"You have a key to the apartment so if anything leaks or a fire breaks out, you can deal with it." I laughed, though I regretted putting it out to the universe.

3

I 'd been on the ferry before. Mom and Dad didn't have a lot of money for travel, but a walk-on was cheap and Vancouver Island was pretty close for a day trip. A ferry had a cafeteria and a gift shop. A shifter-owned boat had neither. Traveling on the Sea Wolf had two huge bene-fits over the ferry. It was fast, and we arrived in the heart of downtown. I figured it was a fair trade.

D slid us into the assigned slip at Quayside Marina and we walked the finger dock to the hotel. We had a suite with a balcony that suited Destroyer as a base camp—his words, not mine.

"I guess we have a few hours," I said after we unpacked in our separate rooms. "We can walk to the meeting with Helena Blackwood, do some reconnaissance."

"I will contact my potential recruits," Destroyer said. "You handle the ground troops."

I passed the instructions on to D.

"I guess the buildings make it difficult for him. Lots of updrafts to fight if he wants to land on the street," D said. He pulled up the map on his phone. "Although the local birds manage. He has a point about trying to talk to an animal, but you can't be seen doing it. I hear people are eccentric here, but talking to a raccoon might do more than just raise some eyebrows."

"There'll be someone in an alley," I said, surprised I didn't even flinch at the idea of talking to a rat. I guess my powers made the animals seem more... not human, but more like individuals.

"We're meeting at the Steam Clock, right?" D tapped in a request for directions.

I checked my phone in case something had changed. "Yes. I don't know what she'll expect of us, but we should eat lunch somewhere before." I didn't want to restrict us to the hotel unless we were actively investigating. There was a real risk that I'd run into a friend from school, so I'd made a charm to change my appearance. Brown hair, still a curly mop, but not red, and my eyes would be gray, not blue.

I slid the charm from its velvet bag. A silver coin with a purple stone in the center. I'd strung it on a leather cord to wear around my neck. I stood in front of the mirror and slipped it over my head. The reflection didn't change. What did I do wrong?

"Wow. You look like a completely different person," D said.

"You should be able to see through it," I said, hiding the relief in my voice. I guess it's not a surprise that I wasn't affected.

He tipped his head to the side and squinted. "Yeah, I still see the disguise, but I can also see you beneath it. Plain humans won't get past the first layer. We good to go?"

I led D to my favorite restaurant in downtown. Not one of the fancy ones because I could never afford them on the pay from my part-time job: Ramen Danbo. Most food was available on Henbane because of kitchen witches, but in my opinion, things like ramen and pho need to be made by experts.

The lineup was short for a change, so D and I were happily slurping noodles within twenty minutes of strolling from our hotel.

"When were you in Vancouver?" I asked him.

"I had to come sit my exams for my tech degree," he said after swallowing his mouthful of heaven. "If it was just about doing the work on Henbane, I wouldn't have bothered, but I need to get the latest news, and that comes to people with degrees. So I came in to UBC, sat the exam, and went home. I guess you could say I haven't really been here."

"We might have some sightseeing time," I said. "After this problem is fixed."

He pushed his bowl away and wiped his face. "Jan needs to come taste this so he can recreate real ramen. I would like to see Capilano Canyon, that bridge sounds fun. And Stanley Park, and... all of it."

We'd need to rent a car, but that should be easy since I had a driver's license. "Let's solve this fast. We should head out so we can wander to Gastown. I hope Helena Blackwood has a private place for us to talk."

We window-shopped along the way, picking out our favorite display and planning which place we'd hit to grab a drink. D bought a T-shirt from one of the big tourist shops on Water Street, and then we stood with a group of tourists waiting for the clock to whistle out the hour. Gastown was its usual busy, noisy self. Cars creeping along Water Street, waiting for construction delays and honking every chance they got. As much as I love the peace on Henbane, the occasional taste of a faster pace was exhilarating.

"Ms. Fortuna?" A tall blonde stepped forward as the

tourists split off to the next destination. She was radiating confidence and irritation in equal parts.

"Helena Blackwood?" I asked even though she'd used my name and who else could she be?

"And your friend?" The way she said that made it sound like I couldn't possibly have friends and had a lot of gall bringing someone else into the situation.

I reminded myself I was the protector and my decisions were always going to keep the world safe.

"Didier Rothtect," D said, holding his hand out to shake. "You can call me D."

She shook his hand and I got the distinct impression she wanted to wipe hers with sanitizer afterward. "You may call me Ms. Blackwood."

"Let's get down to the problem," I said. If she was a sample of the attitude of this council, I wanted to solve the case and get home in as little time as possible.

"Not here, of course," she said with a sigh. "We have a rented office a block away. Please follow me."

She didn't even look to see if we'd obeyed. I mean, we had; it would be ridiculous to hold our ground.

4

The room wasn't the small side office I expected—one that would have three chairs and maybe a desk or coffee table, the kind of rental office you can find anywhere. It was a boardroom. Long table, clearly built in place by a talented witch. Chairs around it, enough for twelve people. And a jug of water and glasses on a credenza under the window.

Six people were already waiting for us. Helena took the seventh seat and gestured for us to sit across from the rest of the people. I stepped into the room and a spell flowed over me.

"What is that?" I asked, trying to keep the panic out of my voice. "You cast a spell without advising us."

D was looking around the room, apparently unworried by the council's action.

"Security," Helena said. "This isn't some secluded island. Here we need to be constantly vigilant. If the business we conduct in this room is ever recorded, it would endanger the lives of every witch and shifter on the planet."

I didn't want to start this relationship with a complaint,

but I imagined what Mrs. V would have said and tried to make it less grumpy. "Do you make it a habit of casting spells on people without their knowledge?"

That put Helena's back up. The spell didn't affect my powers. I could hear Destroyer telling me to put this council in its place. I could see the emotions rising from the group. They were not united, but on this topic, opinions didn't drift far from outright approval.

"We are in the middle of a city filled with plain humans," a woman to Helena's right said. "I accept we should have informed you, but everyone who enters this room is fully aware. I apologize that we didn't think to make you aware."

I glanced at D. He gave me the tiniest of nods. So was he agreeing with them and telling me to move on, or telling me to assert my status and make them feel bad? Or was he saying to make them remove the spell? We were going to have a talk after this to set up some communication system.

"I accept your apology. Please ensure that in the future you do not surprise me with magic again."

Helena agreed for the council. Destroyer was disappointed in my mercy.

"I will be taking notes," D said, pulling out his phone. "The protector will need information and we will not be relying on memory."

Oh, nicely done. Asserted our authority without drama.

"Let me introduce you to the council," Helena said. "From my right, Elizabeth Morrison is the council chair. Robert Kim acts as our vice-chair, Maria Santos, our historian. James O'Brien, Ormand Mistry, and Amalia Svoboda are members at large."

Each of them nodded as their names were mentioned. Elizabeth was short, with dark hair cut in a severe bob. Robert looked like a banker, Maria a lovable grandma,

James a post-grad student—badly trimmed hair, old T-shirt and ancient jeans, Ormand would have fit in at any CEO meeting with his silver hair and expensive suit, and Amalia was the essence of a soccer mom. Great blending-in images.

"And your role?" I asked Helena.

A spike of irritation at being questioned flashed. "I act as the liaison for the community."

"Let's get to business. What exactly is the problem?" I was already yearning to be back on Henbane. I was willing to lose sleep to get this over with.

Maria took over the meeting, pulling out what looked like a fact sheet. So much for nothing being recorded— perhaps she meant audio, not paper.

"A family who recently moved here from Thunder Bay, Ontario, the Reeves—David and Sandra are the parents, and Marcus their son. We have not been able to learn the real reason they left, but it seems Marcus was considered a problem that might be easier to solve in a larger community."

"A child isn't a problem to solve," I said before I could stop myself. "Continue."

Amalia glanced at Maria and said, "I agree, but he does need to be... managed, I suppose. His powers are more... artistic than most of our community. He can create images from people's aspirations, allowing them to see the future they wish for. And he can make art, or I suppose anything, react to his emotions. That is the current problem. He is not responding to the usual training for children to control their powers."

Was that what we did on Henbane? Control children? I didn't think so. I wanted the whole picture before I moved on. "His third power?"

Maria spoke before Amalia could answer. "Kitchen

witch. That power is not the issue. His power affected some graffiti—the one to animate art is. So far, we have not heard of him doing anything with the aspiration power."

D was busy making notes, or that's what I thought until I looked at his screen. "Ask them where the family is now."

Good idea.

"At home," Maria said when I asked. "We have their assurance they won't let Marcus wander until we have a solution."

"I'll need to talk to them," I said. "And did anyone see the graffiti? A plain human, I mean?"

"Two people," Maria said. "A Cory Milton—she is a student at UBC—and Herman Zhang, marketing specialist in Yaletown. Both made videos and posted online."

That was a big problem! I'd met Herman before. My disguise would fool him, but my name was pretty unusual.

"I created bots," James O'Brien said before I could ask about their mitigation actions. "Fake news, AI-generated, anything that would undermine the impact."

"When did this happen?" D asked. "The encounter and the bots?"

"Two days ago, in the evening," Maria said. "The bots were deployed a few hours later, as soon as we were informed."

I looked at D, my tech advisor. "Would the videos be trending?"

"I'll look for them later," he said. "The bots might have made it worse. But time on social media is fickle, so maybe something new is trending now."

I was relieved he didn't insist on searching for the posts. We needed to get out of here with all the information and a way to check on the dynamics of this council. Henbane's leaders didn't all agree, but they presented a unified front.

This group seethed with resentments. That couldn't be good if anyone resisted my solution.

"I will interview the two plain humans after I speak to the Reeves family," I said. "Where can I find them?"

"I will take you to their home," Helena said. "And we have already set up interviews with the two plains."

"When and who do they think I am?" And would I end up having to alter Herman's memories to protect us?

"A marketing specialist," Ormand Mistry said. "I thought that might be a good cover."

"Thank you, I can work with that. Did you give them my name?" Please say no.

"Just your last name," Ormand said. "I thought it would be more credible to sound professional."

Not quite as bad as the whole name. I could pretend to be a cousin or something. "When?"

"Tomorrow," Maria said with an annoyed glance at Ormand. She passed D a sheet of paper. "The locations, times, and what we know of them."

5

The Reeves lived in a small rental house in Strathcona. A good choice for anyone who might be thought of as a little odd. Lots of eccentric artisans and not a lot of people breezing through on their way somewhere else.

Helena knocked on the door and we waited.

"They have been briefed," Helena said. "You shouldn't face any resistance."

Why would they resist someone who was trying to help? And a protector at that? I didn't ask.

The door opened and a man's face was visible through the crack. "Are you alone?"

Helena put her hand out to push the door open farther, but I stopped her. I got the feeling the family didn't trust anyone—okay, obvious to anyone, but I could do something about it. "Mr. Reeves?"

"Are you the protector?" He nodded an answer to my question as he spoke.

"I am. And this is my associate, Didier Rothtect. Can we

come in?" I hoped he didn't ask for ID. I'd have to think about that later. Shouldn't I at least have a business card?

He looked at Helena and then opened the door wider. "Of course."

I turned to Helena before she made a move. "Thank you for bringing us here, but this is protector business and we can find our own way back to the hotel."

The surprise on her face was mirrored by the haze of orange that oozed out of her emotions. I tried to keep my third power from forcing the issue. I wasn't going to be the kind of protector who relied on power. I would prefer collaboration and cooperation. And I couldn't help thinking Phillip might have started on his path of destruction with a few innocent magical nudges.

"Of course," she said, stepping back to give us room. "The council will expect an update tomorrow evening. The sooner this is solved, the better. I will contact you with the time and location."

We watched her walk back to her car and didn't move until she drove around the corner.

"That woman is pretty determined," David said. "Please, come in. We have coffee, tea, water?"

We followed him down a short hall to the kitchen at the back of the house. The footprint of their home was tiny. The first door we passed was open and I saw a couch, coffee table, and a TV. The door opposite was probably a bedroom, a small bathroom came next, then the kitchen. If this was like other houses of the same age that I'd toured, upstairs would be a bedroom and nothing else. Cute heritage homes from early in the last century came with a lot of compromises.

Sandra was sitting at the small pink Formica table. The chairs came from a completely different set because they were turquoise. If it wasn't so worn, the kitchen could have been a model for the fifties retro style.

She had brown wavy hair, fair skin, and a weary aura. David wasn't much better. This crisis was burning them out.

"Where is Marcus?" I asked.

"In his room," David said, pointing to the floor above. "Do you want me to bring him down?"

"No. I'd like to hear your story before we get him worried." The last thing we needed was a volatile kid with emotive magic feeling like he was a problem.

D took a seat and gave me a look that seemed to say 'sit down, you're making everyone nervous.'

"Can I get you anything?" Sandra asked.

I sat beside D and shook my head. "What did you mean about Helena?" I asked David.

"Wait," D said. He pulled out a spell bag and rubbed it to activate the contents. Rose and lilac scents filled the air. Too cloying to be pleasant.

"What are you doing?" Sandra asked, glancing around the room.

"Testing for listening spells and devices," he said. "The council seemed to be paranoid about being spied on. I thought they might have taken precautions here."

"And?" I asked. I remembered the concept of this spell, but there were so many on the list I needed to learn that I had no idea what to look for.

"We're clear," he said. "If there was anything, we'd see a blue glow. So now you know it's safe, you can talk honestly."

I watched the emotions lighting around the Reeves. For them, privacy was a relief. "Let's start. Tell us what we need to know."

David sat on the remaining chair and rubbed his face. A

white aura of fatigue covered his whole body with threads of yellow relief growing to fill the space.

Sandra touched his arm and started talking. "We came here from back east for a fresh start. Marcus got his powers a little late, but we weren't worried. When the council there tested him, we were strongly encouraged to move here, to a large city where there would be more resources."

Okay, I guess I saw the sense in that, and it did seem weird that the council didn't know the details, but I guess people move around all the time without a resume. "Why not Toronto? It was closer."

"The council thought there was a better chance in a completely new environment," David said.

"So you came and settled," D prompted. "Then something happened."

The Reeves shared a glance and I could see they were afraid to tell me the truth.

"If you don't tell me, I can't help." Why was this so hard for them?

"This council accepted us, let us feel safe, and then suggested Marcus would be better off in a... they called it a specialized facility."

"Boarding school," Sandra spat the words. "Marcus overheard. That's when he started having episodes. At first it was just at home. And then he ran away and ended up in an alley downtown before we found him. The graffiti was affected. I don't know who saw it or how the council found out, but they did."

"And then we got the ultimatum," David said. "Marcus goes to the boarding school, or we leave and find another home. Boarding school, my butt. If you have Hogwarts in mind, you are wrong. It's more like a prison."

I couldn't speak for a moment. It didn't make sense. Why

punish a child like that? Why call for help if you'd already made up your mind?

"Why did the council reach out to Mrs. V?" D asked as if he could read my thoughts.

Destroyer grabbed my attention before anyone could answer. I held up a finger to delay them so I could concentrate.

"I will have crows patrol the area." No mention of his army, no imperial tone, just helpful. I shouldn't be suspicious, right?

I told them about my familiar and the crow patrol. "I will know if anyone is acting threatening," I said. "I need to check your backyard before we leave. Sorry to interrupt the flow, why did they ask for a protector?"

"To add credibility," David said. "I'm just guessing, but I think Elizabeth Morrison planned to convince you their idea is the best one."

"I'm not easily convinced," I said. "I'm not sure what solution I'll have, but no child is going to be locked away with my permission. Do you know if there are other children at this school?"

"No," Sandra said. "I'm sure you can get that from Helena or Elizabeth."

I'd certainly be asking a lot of questions at the meeting tomorrow.

D made some final notes. "I don't think this is going to take much time. Will it be a problem to keep Marcus home until we have a solution?"

"No. I'll keep training him," Sandra said. "Please find a way to end this problem soon."

I made that promise. I know I shouldn't have, but I wasn't going to give up.

In the backyard I called for any animals to come talk. A

squirrel showed up in seconds.

"What do you want?" That was different from what I usually got, but I didn't expect city animals to be the same as those on Henbane.

"Can you help keep these witches safe? I can pay with food."

"I have plenty of food and I'm too busy to help you." He twitched his tail and then ran off.

I guess I had to rely on the crow army.

6

I didn't get much sleep. To be fair, D didn't either. We spent most of the night tossing around ideas and discussing the weird feeling we both got from the Vancouver council. It wasn't so much that they had different ideas about how communities would protect themselves. As a community, Vancouver was about the same age as Henbane—not all witches had retreated when the founder created the island. There were plenty of even older communities all over the world. Witches and shifters had been around as long as plain humans.

Unfortunately, history didn't make a council wise. In fact, it could do the opposite. The members would change, but not often. A witch lived a long time, and moving every few decades when your looks didn't match the age you should be didn't bring in new ideas fast enough. The world changed and protection had to evolve with it.

Destroyer wasn't much help. His advice covered the gamut from a revolution to displace the council, all the way to a war to displace the council. He didn't appreciate it when I said that was the same thing.

"You have your first meeting in half an hour," D said when I walked out of the bedroom, showered and dressed and ready for the day—or doing a good job of faking being ready.

"Is my disguise in place?"

Herman Zhang was the one person it had to work on. I wasn't too worried when we were out in public or surrounded by witches. I kept the spell running more to avoid a casual meeting with someone who knew me.

Cossi Fortuna, plain human, had met Herman once. At a party and he'd had too much to drink, but it was a big risk to sit across from him. Unfortunately, the council hadn't thought to give me a fake name when they set up the meeting.

"It's perfect for a plain human. Stop worrying," D said. "What did you decide on if he remembers you?"

"Cousin," I said. "Our mothers wanted to keep the family name going. And I think a touch of my persuasion won't hurt if he doesn't believe me."

I hoped he would believe me, that is. I couldn't help thinking that using my third power to make people obey was the first step to becoming a supervillain. Even if Mrs. V had proven it would only work to protect the magical world, it all felt like good intentions and a particularly dark road.

Herman's office was only a couple of blocks from the hotel, so I could walk.

"I'll wait in the coffee shop," D said. "How about Destroyer—will he be around?"

"I am always around," Destroyer said with a sniff. Who knew crows sniffed?

"Yes," I said, checking my outfit: black silk shirt, black pencil skirt with faint pinstripe of carmine, and black stilettos. "Where's the purse?"

D nodded to the couch. "It's barely big enough for the tablet and your key card."

"I'm a rising star in marketing technology," I said as I put the strap over my shoulder. "Practical is the last thing I should look."

Ten minutes later I was standing in front of the receptionist at Todd and Co, listening to him announce me to Herman.

"Just go on down that hall," he said. "His office is on the right at the end."

I thanked him and followed the directions. The inside didn't match the outside of the building. Yaletown consisted of converted warehouses and office buildings from the 1800s. All brick and tiny windows. Todd and Co was shades of gray—walls, floors, and signage. Like having any personality was offensive to their clients.

Herman showed no hint of recognition when he stood to shake my hand. About my age and good-looking in a sharp way, he had a great smile. "Ms. Fortuna? Thanks for coming in. I have to admit, I'm curious about this whole thing."

"Please, call me Cossi." I figured it was safe to use my name if he had no memory of me. "I represent a marketing research firm that's been contracted to evaluate the effectiveness of experimental advertising techniques."

"The graffiti thing in the alley? That was an ad?" His interest was an intense shade of blue and blasted out the scent of leather.

"Interactive street art campaign. My client is exploring whether dynamic, responsive advertising generates more user engagement than traditional static displays." I'd memorized a bunch of technical terms to prepare.

Herman leaned forward, interested. "Your company? You didn't mention it."

"It's a Japanese firm, but I have been asked to keep details confidential. You know how quickly people jump on a new idea. We'd like to keep this ours for as long as possible."

"Yeah, that's almost the hardest part, right? Keep ahead. So, dynamic how? The stuff I saw didn't look like any projection technology I know about."

Of course he'd actually understand enough about technology to ask informed questions. This was why I was terrible at deception—I always forgot to account for other people being smart. D was right to drill me in what sounded like nonsense last night.

"That's proprietary, obviously. But I can tell you it involved a combination of thermochromic materials and embedded micro-projectors." I was coming to the end of D's lessons.

"Huh. Interesting." He made a note on his pad. "And you're measuring success by social media response?"

"Exactly. User-generated content, sharing frequency, viral potential. The fact that you captured it and posted to social media tells us the campaign was effective at generating immediate response."

"Posted it?" Herman looked confused. "I didn't post anything."

My heart skipped. "The video you recorded?"

"I recorded it, yeah, but I didn't share it anywhere. Too weird. I figured someone would say I faked it." He pulled out his phone. "I still have it though, if you want to see."

I forced myself to stay calm while my brain started racing. If Herman hadn't posted his video, who had? And where were the other videos Helena had mentioned? Was this another lie, or had something else happened that I didn't know about?

"That would be very helpful," I said, trying to sound like I was happy he kept it.

Herman found the video and handed me his phone. The footage was exactly as Helena had described—graffiti that moved and morphed on its own, clearly magical in origin. But the timestamp showed it was recorded four days ago, not two like I'd been told.

"Herman, when exactly did you see this?" I pretended to make a note on my tablet.

"Tuesday night, around eight PM. Why?" He relaxed back in his chair.

Maybe I'd misunderstood the times Helena gave me, but I thought it was Wednesday. "Just confirming our timeline," I said, handing back his phone while trying to look professional instead of confused and slightly angry. "It's important to keep track of how long the effect lasts. Can you tell me about the experience? What you thought when you saw it?"

"Honestly? I thought I was losing my mind. Or someone was playing an elaborate prank. I mean, paint doesn't just move on its own, right?" He grinned in that self-deprecating way I remembered from university. "But then I thought, okay, if this is some kind of viral marketing thing, it's actually pretty clever."

"What did you do afterwards?" I had to play like I was doing the job of an analyst. What I wanted to do was call Helena and confront her over the timing.

"Went home, showed the video to my roommate. He said it was obviously fake, probably some viral marketing thing. Which, turns out he was right." His expression brightened. "So what's next? Do I get to be in a commercial or something?"

I spent another twenty minutes asking questions and subtly probing his memory of the event. The good news was that he seemed completely ready to accept the marketing explanation and move on with his life. The bad news was that everything Helena had told me was wrong, and I was beginning to understand why Mrs. V had warned me about mainland communities and their methods.

I met D at the coffee shop. It was too crowded for us to talk, so we called an Uber and headed out to UBC for the meeting with Cory Milton. Destroyer said he'd pass on joining us because he had emperor business.

When we arrived, D headed for a table near the counter, and I took one close by. He could hear us without being obvious. There was no one else in the Starbucks.

Five minutes later, I had a latte in front of me and a woman walked through the door and looked around. She wore cargo shorts, a BLM T-shirt, and Birkenstocks.

"Are you Cossi?" she asked as she approached my table.

I nodded and asked if she'd like a coffee.

"Cory Milton," she said, extending a hand with a friendly smile. "I'm pretty caffeined out. This is just easy to find, right?"

"Thanks for meeting me. I know you're busy with classes." I shook her hand, grateful that she seemed more excited than suspicious. "I guess if you don't know the campus, it is a good landmark."

"This is about that weird art thing, right? My friends think I'm making it up." She settled into the chair across from me. "I mean, it was pretty amazing, even if it was completely impossible."

"Tell me what you saw," I said, pulling out my tablet to look official while internally crossing my fingers that her story wouldn't complicate the situation any more.

According to Cory, it had happened Monday night, not Tuesday or Wednesday. So it wasn't likely I'd misunderstood

Helena. Someone was lying, and there was no reason for Herman or Cory to do that.

"I was using my GPS to meet friends at this new bar downtown," she said, "but you know how GPS can be in the city. Took a wrong turn and ended up in this alley instead."

I nodded like I understood, though honestly my sense of direction was so bad that GPS usually just made me more confused.

"I heard voices," she continued. "A woman and a man having what sounded like a family discussion. You know, the kind where parents are trying to figure out what to do about something important. When I got closer to ask if I was going the right way, I saw this incredible thing—paint flowing on the wall like it was alive."

Sandra and David were there? Talking about family problems in an alley? Yes, they had said Marcus ran away. Was I going to suspect everyone of lying?

"All humans lie," Destroyer answered. "That is why animals are superior."

I ignored him. "What were the parents discussing?" Maybe their conversation would give me a clue about what was really happening here.

"The woman was saying maybe they should find some-where quieter to live, a smaller community where things would be more manageable. The man was arguing they should give Vancouver more time, that big cities had more resources for kids with special needs." Cory's eyes darkened with the memory. "My folks kind of did that when I told them I wanted to become a biologist. They wanted an archi-tect, I loved plants. We worked it out."

Her emotions were all flowing together, like her memory and her empathy were getting blended. "Cory, did you record any of this?"

"I tried to, but my phone kept acting up. The screen would go all weird and glitchy every time I pointed it at the wall." She shrugged like it was a normal occurrence for technology to have tantrums. "Probably just needed an update or something. My phone's always doing weird stuff."

Or magical interference, I thought but didn't say. "Have you been back to the alley since then?"

"Yeah, yesterday. I brought my friend Mike to show him where it happened, but the graffiti was totally normal again. Just regular spray paint. Mike thinks I dreamed the whole thing."

I thanked her and waited for Cory to leave before I joined D.

"The council has a lot to explain," D said.

7

D and I sat at the small kitchen table in our suite. I'd picked up a large notebook in the UBC bookstore because having our notes scattered between computers, phones, and tablets was making everything feel more chaotic. I needed to put some order to the lies.

"Okay, let's draw out the timeline as far as we know it," D said, opening the book and drawing a line from top to bottom. "What's the start day?"

There were some options. Did this start when we got the call? When the Reeves came to Vancouver? When the graffiti was seen?

"Let's start with the earliest day someone said they saw the magic," I said. "And I guess the end date will be what? The day we solve it?"

D shook his head and clicked his pen onto a different colored ink. "It's not for a record of the investigation. We'll leave room for more, but I think getting all the data straight up to now will help."

"Okay, let's start with Cory. She's the first one to see what happened." At least I believed her. I should have asked Mark to come, maybe along with D. Mark would have known who was lying right away. My ability to do that was tied to emotions, and it looked like the council had better shields than I thought.

D wrote her name in red ink and put Monday beside it. "Do we know any more?"

"The Reeves were there," I said. "Did they mention it?"

He checked his notes. "Yes. Not the argument, but that makes sense. They found him in the alley."

"So Cory must have seen the effect of his magic just after it happened. I wonder why Sandra or David didn't deactivate it."

D wrote that question on a separate sheet. "We'll ask. And I'll list the lies. The timings, the posting. Oh, and that means there are no bots, right?"

And the plain humans couldn't shield their emotions. That's why I believed them!

"You just figuring that out now?" Destroyer asked. I imagined him rolling his eyes. "Should I abandon my army and babysit you?"

"No. I need you out there watching," I thought at him.

"Cossi?" D said.

"Just talking to the mighty Destroyer. Lies. I think the only ones we know about are the council's. Plain humans can't shield. So everything any of the council members said is suspect."

D wrote four more items on his list. The school, the options for keeping Marcus safe, the potential solutions. "Herman's timing is Wednesday, and he didn't post. I guess we'll put that the magic went away the day after Herman's encounter."

"It could have been earlier, but that will work." I looked over his shoulder. Using different colors for each person helped to point out the inconsistencies. "So the timeline kind of backs up the plain humans' stories. Let's plug in what the council said."

"Both encounters were on Tuesday, and we know neither happened that night. Bots launched on Wednesday—well, that's what James said." There was no reason for them, so another lie.

We needed a solution and I wanted to deal with this council lying to me, but Marcus was the priority. I don't know if I had any authority over council rules anyway. "What are the options?" I asked D and Destroyer. "We need to include the boarding school idea, too. Not that I'm going to let them lock him up."

"The crows suggest a protective team. There are sufficient numbers pledging allegiance that we can follow him wherever he wishes to go."

I told D.

"Sure, having a murder of crows floating around him all the time won't look weird or anything," he said.

"Is there a way to get crows to look at this school?" It was worth a try. Maybe the birds would see happy kids.

"We require a location and time to fly there," Destroyer said. "So the answer is yes, but I think it will be too late."

I agreed and asked Destroyer to continue to make sure the family was safe.

"We could suppress his powers," D said. "We might not come up with an answer we're completely happy with."

"Put it down," I said. "My parents agreed to do that with me, so we know it's not harmful. And add relocation as an option. And intensive training to control his power. It would be better to let him learn to use it rather than bind it."

"On Henbane he will be under the protection of my

imperial guard," Destroyer said. "It is the safest part of my realm."

That was the same thing I'd been thinking, almost to the word. Was Destroyer just parroting back my own idea?

"What about Henbane?" I asked D. "Is it possible? Are there rules about moving there?"

"What does your instinct say?" he asked. "As the protector, you should know the right answer. I'm not talking about rules. You should know which one is the right choice."

"I guess I should call Mrs. V to make sure we cover any requirements." I didn't bother to tell him that I hadn't trusted the little voice that told me to take the family to Henbane, and it was only when my familiar said it that I knew it was right. I really needed to work on this confidence thing. Faking it wasn't leading to being it.

Mrs. V answered on the first ring. "Have you solved the problem?"

I told her the whole story. The council's lies, the family problems, the choice to bring them to Henbane, and that it felt like the right decision.

"You cannot solve every problem by filling Henbane," she said, but there was no sting in her tone. "I will make sure the rest of our council is ready. You need to listen to the Vancouver one or you'll be fighting them every step of the way. When?"

"Tonight, unless the Reeves need time to prepare," I said. "We're meeting with the council in a couple of hours. I can't see any of their options working, especially when we can't rely on their word. Should I confront them?"

I heard the chuckle on the other end of the line. I hoped it wasn't at the idea of me confronting anyone. "Be careful," she said. "Yes, you need to let them know you caught the... call them discrepancies, but don't do anything about it. If they have an excuse or apologize, accept it. I have a feeling you'll be working with them again soon."

I hoped it would be a long time, but I agreed. She told us to bring the Sea Wolf to the main dock and to call her when we left Vancouver.

"I will be delegating my authority in preparation to leave," Destroyer said.

I thought about mentioning past empires that stretched beyond what they could control, but let him to it.

8

I sat facing the council members in the same boardroom as before. Destroyer was giving me running encouragement to order the witches into submission and demand obedience. I tuned him out because he wouldn't stop when I asked.

D sat beside me with his tablet on the table. If we needed to show proof for any of what we'd found, he had it teed up. And he was recording, but we'd decided to keep that to ourselves.

"Ms. Fortuna," Elizabeth said. "I hope you have information for us to help decide on the next steps with the Reeves child."

"I still have some outstanding questions," I said with more confidence than I actually felt. No one mentions how hard the fake-it-till-you-make-it part is. "In our investigations we found a few... inconsistencies. The timeline for instance, and the fact that no one posted videos to social media."

Elizabeth exuded a bruise-plum-colored embarrassment —maybe not for what they did, but for getting caught? "Perhaps we weren't as precise as we could have been on the timing."

"I can understand in the rush to protect the community you may become a little confused," I said. "But James said he deployed bots to undermine the posting."

I let that sit and watched the emotions of the whole council. There was definitely a split, but everything over-lapped so it was impossible to assign the emotions to the individual. More embarrassment, anger, smugness, and real fear. The whole mix carried the aroma of raw wine.

Helena cleared her throat and glared around at the council, taking command of the situation instead of the chairwitch. Now that was interesting. "The situation was dire in our opinion. You have no idea how fragile the veil is that keeps us safe."

When caught in a lie, go on the attack. Nice. "I grew up in Vancouver, so I have a good idea of the problem. I'm not here to discuss that issue. I have another question to clarify the last of the details before I give my decision." That surprised everyone. They really thought I'd let them decide what to do after lying to the protector? I channeled my inner Mrs. V—less grouchy, but still in charge. As I did, I realized I was no longer faking it. I knew what I was doing would protect the magical community. "This boarding school. Explain how it would help."

Elizabeth touched Helena's hand and took over the meeting. Somehow she'd managed to shield her emotions, and my confidence dipped.

"It is fairly isolated, so there would be little danger as the boy learns to control his magic. He will return to his parents when he can prove he has improved. I'm sure he will only be gone for a couple of years."

Did she really think that was acceptable? "How many

children are currently living there?" My question prompted a spike of anxiety from Robert Kim, vice chair, and no friend of Elizabeth's.

"It is a new facility," Elizabeth said. "Marcus would be the only student for a while. We certainly hope there is no spate of difficult children to fill the halls."

I'd heard enough, and so had Destroyer. "I would not allow one of my subjects to be so isolated."

"Very well. In light of all that has happened to date, my decision is to take the Reeves family to Henbane. They will be welcome to stay as long as they like. Marcus will join the classes with other children his age."

"But that is not what we intended," Maria blurted out, her angry emotions reaching toward me.

I listened to Destroyer babble on in my mind and D's silence beside me. He wasn't there as muscle, but he did a pretty good impression of someone who would protect me.

The room went quiet. Maria the only one who voiced an objection, and perhaps the only council member really unhappy with my decision based on the emotions around me. I let the silence carry on because I tried to understand why she wanted to send the boy away. My solution took him to a safe place. He'd get the education he needed. His parents could settle somewhere accepting.

Just as I was about to speak, Robert Kim said, "And what of the benefit the boy will bring to his community when his powers are fully realized?"

I looked at D, hoping he had a hint on how to respond. This was all about exploiting a child? D leaned in to whisper. "Shut them down now. If you engage with him, they will see it as weakness."

"Disband them and replace this troublesome council

with others," Destroyer all but yelled at me. "My army is ready to stand at your side."

I held up my hand to stop him from overwhelming my attention. Yeah, I know he couldn't see it, but he got the message. And the council members thought the gesture was aimed at them.

I stood. The best way to end a conversation was to leave. "My decision is what matters. You called for the protector and I came. I will speak to the Reeves and make arrangements to transport them."

D led me through the door and I waited until we were on the street before I took a breath. My body was shaking with adrenaline and a remnant of the fury that I fought to contain in the meeting.

"Keep walking," D said, taking my arm. "We don't want to be here when they exit. I'm texting David Reeves as we walk."

I focused on moving. We made it halfway back to the hotel when David Reeves responded to D's text.

"They need time to get ready to go. Marcus is happy, so they want to move quickly."

"Tell them to meet us in the hotel lobby tomorrow at nine," I said.

9

T he next morning, at 9:30, we piled into the Sea Wolf and informed Mrs. V we were on our way. D used his weather power to add a little speed— not a tailwind like I thought, but he cleared any rough water ahead of us. I was looking forward to lunch at Jan's. We were all crowded into the small covered space, not a cabin by any means. I didn't want anyone in the family to arrive without some knowledge—I'd done that and it wasn't great.

Before I could start telling them what my home was like, Marcus asked, "What's Henbane like? Will people be afraid of me there too?"

Sandra pulled him into a hug. "I'm sure it will be fine," she said. "It's all witches and shifters, so no plain humans to worry about."

"I've never seen a shifter," Marcus said. "Are they nice?"

"Shifters look like us most of the time," I said. "Even on Henbane, they don't usually shift in public unless there's a real need. It's nice to be away from the plain humans, but we are all people."

"Where will we live?" Sandra asked. "I heard there were no hotels."

"Where does your information come from?" D asked.

Good question. The only off-island witches I'd met were at the festival last week—was it really only a couple of days in the past? They all seemed to have a good idea what our life was like, but then, most of them had relatives or friends on Henbane.

"The councils," David said. "Thunder Bay and Vancouver. No one seemed to know much for sure, and it's hard to imagine being in such a safe place."

Part of being a secret island, I guess. Now that D and I brought them, the Reeves would be able to leave and come back without an escort.

"You'll find a permanent place," D said. "I guess Cossi is going to offer rooms at The Inner Spell to start?"

I'd sent a text to Zinnia right after Mrs. V, asking her to prepare some rooms. "I opened a retreat earlier this year. We haven't booked up yet, so you should be comfortable." Mrs. V and the council would probably want to greet our newcomers.

"I don't want to be a burden," David said. "Is there work? I can turn my hand to most things."

I let D explain the details on that side. I thought at Destroyer, who was perched on the bow of the boat like he owned the world. "Can you reach Tulip from here?"

"Not yet, but soon. What orders do you wish me to communicate?"

I laughed at the idea of the little lynx thug taking orders. "Just to have Mrs. V avoid an interrogation at the dock. They need a day or two to rest and explore the island."

"I will inform you when the message is received. I have no way to enforce your order."

Even Destroyer, Emperor of the World, couldn't get Tulip to be nice. I felt better about my lack of skill in that aspect. "Fine."

The conversation had continued while I made the arrangements. David was talking over his skills with Sandra and D. Marcus was looking at my familiar, his emotions all warm apricot.

"Will I get one?" he asked me when he noticed I was watching.

"A familiar? They pick you, so I don't know. How are you feeling about the move?" His emotional aura flickered to icy green as his attention moved from Destroyer. "Excited and worried."

"Worry is kind of part of the excitement," I said. "You will be fine, I'm sure."

"Tulip reports Mrs. V asking what you thought was going to happen?" Destroyer announced. "I will remind you that I am not a messenger."

10

We docked and I saw a welcoming committee standing at the foot of Main Street. Not just Mrs. V as I'd hoped, but Jan and Jeffery, too. Main was never crowded, but I got the feeling people were staying away. And Tulip was nowhere near the dock.

"Don't worry," I said to Sandra. "They aren't here to send you back."

"How did you know?" she asked.

Well, the look on her face was easy to read, but I had my power to rely on. "I can read emotions. You can't believe it's over. Kind of waiting for the other shoe to drop thing. David is cautious, Marcus is excited."

"What if he does something?" she asked. "Something they don't like?"

I patted her arm, knowing my words wouldn't have much effect on her until she'd been here a while. "I know this is weird, but I think they'd be delighted to have him demonstrate his power. You'll see that we celebrate here and don't punish. That's my mentor, Mrs. V, and one of our kitchen witches, Jan—he runs a bistro—and Jeffery is another member of our council."

As I pointed them out, Zinnia came running from the bike park. "And that's the person managing The Inner Spell, where you'll be staying."

We headed up the ramp as soon as D tied off the boat. Destroyer headed to the forest to take command back from his lieutenant. I didn't bother to comment.

Jeffery stepped forward and held out his hand. "Welcome to Henbane. We'll head to Jan's for a bite and introductions."

My stomach grumbled at his words. Sure, the food had been great, but nothing beat Jan's food, except maybe Sheena's or Zoe's. They each provided a different vibe: relaxed, hearty, and comforting in that order.

When we were seated in the empty bistro, Jan explained he'd closed for the day so we had privacy. He brought out a feast of pizza and salad along with beer, wine, and milk.

"Thank you for taking us in," David said. "It's a bit overwhelming to be wanted."

Mrs. V handed him a plate and a beer. "The Vancouver council doesn't know what's good for them. An artist and a kitchen witch would be welcome even without being able to make images. Your powers are weak, though. Why?"

She didn't modify the grouchiness much, but it almost sounded kind to my ears.

"We've been so involved with Marcus," Sandra said, closing her eyes to concentrate on her magic. "I didn't notice before. They've kind of retreated, right?"

"We'll fix that up in the morning," Jeffery said, poking at his salad. "Tomorrow Doc Rene will head out and give you a check over. What are your powers, just so she'll know what to look for?"

Marcus wasn't with us, so his parents were less guarded in their reactions. He'd happily followed Jan into the kitchen discussing recipes. I could see suspicion spike and then fold into a shield around David and Sandra. She sighed and touched David's hand. "Sorry, I guess we need to work on trust. I'm an earth witch with a talent for herbs, a healer, and a cloth magician."

David smiled at her and I wondered if Doc Rene had any experience in trauma medicine. Although if Sandra was a healer... Not my job to interfere. They would need to manage their own integration.

"My powers are music, animal breeding, and potions," David said. "It will be nice to stop ignoring our callings."

Zinnia raised her glass to toast the newcomers. "How delightful. I'm looking forward to chatting with you about everything. And I have an idea that I'll need to talk to other witches about, but if they agree, I think you'll be of huge value to us."

The committee. Zinnia wanted more than just her voice for the mainlander communities. I'd back her on the idea, and maybe that would free me up a bit for my protector duties.

Marcus came back into the room and lights started to swirl around us like Jan had installed a disco ball. "Jan said I could help him cook if it's okay with you," he said. "Can I, please?"

Sandra and David froze. The shield snapping back into place.

"Jeffery," Zinnia said. "Let's dance. Can someone make music? Oh, what fun we'll have!"

She pulled Jeffery from his seat and twirled around.

David relaxed, waved a hand, and suddenly "Dancing Queen" started playing from thin air. It took Sandra longer to accept what was happening. Then she laughed and pulled her husband to the dance floor Jan made by pushing tables to the walls.

"We'll take that as a yes," Jan said to Marcus. "You'll settle in first, right? Meet the other kids, attend school for a week so you know what's expected?"

"Yes, anything. I have some great ideas for a dessert. I like those best." The boy's eyes were wide at the sight of his parents acting as though they had no cares.

The meeting only lasted an hour. By the end of it, the Reeves family were exhausted. The acceptance cracking open all the fear of the last days.

"We'll settle in," Zinnia said. "It's a bit of a bike to the retreat. Do you need help?"

"We get to ride again?" Marcus asked, looking up at his parents.

"We didn't bring our bikes," David said. "I guess we're walking."

"Just take them from the parking area," Zinnia said. "Dolph had a shifter move your luggage to your room. There are so many people you need to meet. I'm thrilled to introduce you to your new life."

She took them out of the bistro, chattering all the way. I started clearing the table.

"You did the right thing," Mrs. V said. "Now you know you can trust your instincts."

I wasn't as sure as she was, but my stupid inner critic didn't chime in, so I'd take that as a win.

11

I woke up the next morning to the dawn chorus of birds. For everyone else it was chirping and tweeting as the flocks greeted the day. For me it was a litany of complaints and gossip. I was so happy to hear that after missing it on the mainland that I jumped out of bed and started breakfast without my usual desire for a snooze button on the world.

Today I had a purpose and I was going to get some answers. The next time I headed off Henbane, I needed to be armed with a lot more knowledge.

I texted Mrs. V that I was coming over. If she wanted a more decisive Cossi, she'd have to be okay with me telling her rather than asking for permission. Okay, I had to talk myself into it and I admit to waiting for her to reprimand me.

She sent back a thumbs up. Because she was agreeing to the meeting? Or because she was so mad at my impertinence that she couldn't type out words? Sure, I thought I'd gained confidence with the resolution of the Vancouver problem, but something about Mrs. V kept sending me back to the day I found out I was a witch and had no clue what to do. I'd done a lot since then, but I kept regressing when I was with her. I guess that's the next thing for me to work on.

I stopped at Jan's where I found Marcus happily explaining the process he used to make the tray of pastries on the bar. So much for waiting to settle in. I guess kids do bounce back fast.

I didn't care how he made a dozen perfectly identical pastry cones filled with cream and fruit. I bought two, ordered coffee and tea, and wondered if I should put Marcus on the list of food vendors for the retreat. His eyes lit up and I was swamped in a whirling mist of rainbows after placing the order. Perhaps controlling his power was more important right now.

"Have you met your teacher?" I asked him.

"Mom and Dad wanted to go first, so Jan said I could cook," Marcus said.

"The kid is going to make everyone fat," Jan said with a grin. "What he can do without training is crazy. Like me, Sheena, and Zoe are good at food, Marcus is a genius."

The kid blushed, but the bistro walls shimmered in a coating of gilt.

"Lessons first," I said. "You have no idea how much there is to learn about Henbane."

I left them and took my treats with me. I hadn't even thought about Sandra and David's expectations. Yes, meeting the teacher was a good way to feel like Marcus would be nurtured and give her an idea of where he was in magic and just plain subjects. I had a good feeling they'd settle fast.

Mrs. V was sitting in the kitchen as usual. Tulip, looking twice the size she'd been a few days ago, was curled up under the chair.

I put the treats on the table and automatically went to the cupboard for plates, cutlery, and mugs. "Marcus is already working in the kitchen," I said. "And he's not even a little worried about throwing his art magic around."

"Good. Now we have business." She glanced at Tulip and the lynx stalked off to her corner like she was hunting prey.

"You've come to an understanding?" I asked as I served the food.

"We both want to stay here, so she has agreed to learn," Mrs. V said. "And I have talked to Elias about some expansion plans. It's not really fair to keep her confined to this little cottage."

She took a bite of the pastry and her features softened. "This takes me back to my childhood. Not that I had anything like this, but somehow it evokes nostalgia. That boy is going to be an asset. Now, what do you want to talk about?"

I tasted my own cream horn before answering. I closed my eyes and I was back in our home in Vancouver before my mom died. The fire blazing and the aroma of roasting vegetables floating from the kitchen, and a mug of hot chocolate in my hands.

"Wow!" I returned to the present with no regret, just a feeling of being loved. I refused to be distracted from my goal. "A couple of things. I guess, mostly about why I've never seen kids up to now and what the protector role is all about, and will I meet the others?" Dropping it all on her gave Mrs. V a chance to pick her topic.

"The easiest to answer is about the children," she said after another bite. "There aren't many, and their studies are concentrated. Mostly they stick to the school and home. With Marcus arriving, I think we have twenty children or a few more, of varying ages. This younger generation needs to get busy on procreation."

I ignored the comment. There were plenty of people my age around. They could take care of multiplying until I understood my role. "It sounds like there are parts of the island I haven't been allowed to see." Not too much of a surprise—during the festival I'd found out about the farms.

"As protector, it will all open up to you," Mrs. V said. "We didn't want to overwhelm you."

She hadn't shielded her emotions and I read that there was more. I wasn't going to let that slide.

"That's not entirely the truth," I said. "You might as well tell me. I can't be a good protector without knowing the whole story."

She glared at me, but it was just for show. "We hid parts of the island when you arrived. For their protection and yours. Now that spell has been lifted."

"Okay, I get it. But you need to tell me about the protectors now. I didn't know there were others until I became one. How did you manage when you don't leave Henbane? How big an area do I need to cover?" I ran out of steam, not questions.

"I can't tell you everything all at once because it's too big," she said, glancing over at Tulip. "The easy answers. There were a hundred protectors last century, but the numbers have been dwindling. It's not considered a crisis— it's happened before. Now there are ten. Four, including you, are new and the rest are more like me, a hundred years or more of experience. You are not assigned an area beyond your local communities. When a need arises without one of us near, the communities reach out to me. I know where all of us are. And I have not had anything complex to handle that couldn't be solved by a phone call or Zoom meeting."

I took another bite of my pastry, needing a boost of comfort as I absorbed that information.

"We are more important when there are few of you," Destroyer told me. "You must strive to be their leader."

"I can barely manage my own responsibilities," I replied.

"Tulip tells me we should not threaten your mentor," he said. "I will return to my business."

The conversation had taken place in my mind, but by Mrs. V's expression, Tulip told her everything.

"Don't worry," she said. "I suppose you should know that your familiar is correct. My plan is to train you to replace me."

12

I would be the, what? Head protector? Even now, well before it would happen, the weight of the responsibility threatened to suffocate me. "Really? I barely know the witch world. And what about shifters? I haven't learned much at all about them. And since I keep getting surprised by facts that everyone seems to know, are there other magical creatures?"

Destroyer laughed in my mind. "You do not need to be afraid. You have the emperor of the world at your side."

This time his ego didn't cheer me up.

Mrs. V gave Tulip a stern look and I really didn't want to know why. I assumed it was something about getting rid of the liability named Cossi Fortuna.

She turned to me and sighed. "I am not about to move on to the next life. There is plenty of time for you to learn what you need."

"When?" I couldn't wait for the right opportunity for lessons. There was no guarantee that time would ever come.

"I will answer one of your questions now, and then I

think you need to meet with the Reeves. They are almost as lost in this world as you were when you arrived."

I couldn't argue with that, but I needed one answer that could be clear, and I'd already asked the question. "Are there other magical beings?"

"The world is big, and we do not know all of it. In my lifetime I have never heard of anything but shifters and witches. That is the best I can do."

Okay, I could accept that as a probably no. I mean, she'd crafted her reply specifically to shut me up. Sure, she'd spent most of her time here on Henbane, but I can't believe anyone would keep other magical people a secret from the head of the protectors.

I took the plates and mugs to the sink and washed them as I thought about the Reeves. I did need to find out how they got along with the teacher—I should know who that is. While I was on Henbane, I had a list of tasks for myself. It was unacceptable for a protector not to know the people she worked with.

"Take them with you," Mrs. V said. "A very good plan. Start with the council members—that will help them see how differently we think."

"Destroyer, stop relaying my thoughts through Tulip," I thought at him.

"Then stop trying to hide your thoughts from your mentor."

Mrs. V chuckled. "As I have learned, familiars don't take orders."

Probably best that they didn't, I thought. "Then the committee?" I said, returning to our plans. "Zinnia thought they might help out with finding a solution."

"That is good—you can take a few days to get them oriented to the island as you go. And I have some reading material for you. Histories to answer some questions, and probably provoke more."

My education had focused on magic up to now, so maybe I'd find the new books more entertaining.

My phone rang while I was up to my arms in soapy water. Mrs. V looked at the screen. "Helena Blackwood." She answered the call and put it on speaker, putting her fingers to her lips.

I almost said the call was being monitored for quality control, but didn't think Helena would get the joke. "What can I do for you?" I dried my hands and joined Mrs. V at the table as I talked.

"We have a situation," Helena said. "Your presence is needed in Manning Park as soon as you are able to get here."

I made eye contact with Mrs. V, but she shook her head. Neither of us had any notice from our powers. Of course, I didn't know if that happened anyway.

"What is the situation?" I wasn't going to rush up to Manning Park to solve a disagreement between council members.

"After you left, some of the council members advocated for a retreat. We were shocked to learn how different your thinking was from ours. So we came here. One of our members was found dead in her room. We have contained the situation for now, but at some point the plain humans will get suspicious. How soon can you be here?"

The whole thing came across as an order. And Helena knew the answer to her own question, more or less. There was no teleportation spell. I needed to arrange for the boat again, or be stuck with the ferry, and then the drive from Vancouver to Manning Park.

"I will make arrangements and text you." I ended the call.

"We have an SUV in Sechelt," Mrs. V said. "And in Vancouver."

I pulled up my maps program and searched a few choices. "We have time to get the ferry and drive straight through. Bypassing Vancouver gains us an hour. I'm not sure what steps they've taken to hide the crime, but I would have put out the do not disturb sign and a spell to cover any odors."

"Take Mark," she said, giving me no feedback on my suggestion.

"I'll ask him. What about our plans for the Reeves? Not that I'm going to delay for that, but someone still needs to take them around."

"Leave it with me," she said. "Go make your arrangements. It's up to you, but I wouldn't text Helena Blackwood back until you are on the road. I don't like her attitude and it will do her good to worry for a while."

I grinned because that was totally my plan. It wasn't petty. She was disrespecting the role of protector. "I'll give you an update when I know more," I said, "and probably reach out for advice."

"You have more experience than I do in solving murders," she said without any sarcasm. "I will help where I can."

"Do not leave me behind," Destroyer ordered me. "I will suffer the indignity of a travel cage to ensure I am at your side."

13

It was easy for Mrs. V to say take Mark—he was the cop after all—but in the past he'd run his own investigation. My team was Lilibeth, Lance, and D. I needed them all. Unfortunately for me, they weren't at my beck and call. All of them had jobs that had nothing to do with me.

"Tell them what you want," Destroyer said. "You are the protector!"

"Not a dictator," I thought back at him. "And my power isn't telling me I need everyone."

I headed for Run, Fly, Slither, Lilibeth's pet store and familiar boarding place. I needed a travel cage and advice.

When I explained, Lilibeth pulled a generously sized cage from a back room. "For the ferry," she said. "Cover it with a sheet or something light and he won't be noticed."

"The fumes?" The parking deck was not so bad during the trip because being open on both ends gave a cleansing breeze. It did reek of diesel and gasoline, which made me queasy.

"I will endure," Destroyer said. "I will require water and food."

I passed his comment to Lilibeth. "I can put a filter spell on the cover, and there's a water feeder in the cage. He doesn't need food on the ferry—it's only forty minutes at sea—so an hour and a half if you cover him before you get to the gate, and then you can stop and let him free for the drive."

It was a better option than the pet area. Although Destroyer would probably have an army of maltipoos by the time we docked.

"Will you come?" I didn't have time to dance around an explanation about why I needed help.

"I don't have anyone to look after the animals," she said. "Hang on, we'll call Lance and D, and Mark? Then you don't have to waste time talking to all of us individually."

I loved the fact she didn't question my need. In less than a minute we had our call set up and I explained about the murder, the council, everything I could. D chimed in about the attitude of the council.

"I can come," Mark said right away. "Nothing criminal going on here, and it's not like this will take more than a day or two, right?"

"I hope not. I'm not looking forward to being isolated with that group of witches for days." I crossed my fingers that I didn't just jinx us, if that was even a thing.

"Someone needs to look after the new family," Lance said.

"I was thinking of asking Zinnia," I said. "She's already working with them."

"She's too new," Lilibeth said. "Since I can't leave, I'll work with the family. Maybe one of them will find a familiar."

Lilibeth loved it when witches matched with animals. It wasn't a common event—the animal chose the witch. Seems fair enough since the animal felt everything the witch did and died when they died.

"Thanks," I said. "They are facing a lot of change."

"Dolph won't let me leave Henbane," Lance said. "I'll be here on the end of a call or text, but I'm stuck."

I was pretty sure I could convince Dolph to change his mind, but I didn't have time to track him down.

"D? You know the council, are you okay with coming?" I might need his powers too. A little rain might keep the plain humans inside when we needed to talk to animals. And Manning Park was a long way from cell towers, so I wasn't sure how accessible anyone would be by phone.

"I'm in. How about we meet at the Main Street dock in twenty? That should have us on the ferry early enough for us to miss the rush hours."

We agreed and I grabbed the cage and hurried across the street to my apartment. Lance would be in soon to open the bookstore. I'd made the right decision to hand over the running of my two businesses to managers. Otherwise, I'd never be able to leave in a hurry.

I packed a bag with essentials: clothes, toiletries, and road snacks. I filled the water bottle in Destroyer's cage and one for me. I looked at the teas in the kitchen, which I'd spent hours testing and labeling. Ingredients would be hard to get at the scene. I placed tins of sleep, think, and nourish into my backpack. That would have to do.

D and Mark were waiting for me outside the front door. We headed down to the dock, where we took one of the community boats to Sechelt, where we picked up the RAV4. Destroyer hopped into the cage as we approached the ferry terminal and I threw the bespelled cover over him.

Luck was with us—we were the last car on the ferry.

14

The drive from the ferry terminal to Manning Park took about three hours, which gave me plenty of time to worry about what we were going to find when we got there. A dead council member was definitely more serious than a kid with artistic magic, and I had a feeling the Vancouver council's approach to "containing the situation" was going to be as problematic as everything else they'd done.

"At least it's not in the middle of downtown," D said as we wound through increasingly rural roads. "Easier to keep plain people away from magical problems."

"True," Mark said from the passenger seat. "I'm not sure how long they'll be able to hide the body behind spells, but I'm sure we need to move fast."

I tried not to think about those complications. From his perch on the back seat beside me, I could see Destroyer's impatience glowing from his small body.

"How much longer?" he asked in my mind. "Should I leave you here and fly to this lodge?"

"Almost there and we're still moving faster than you can

fly," I told him. "Please remember, these aren't your crows. Don't order them around."

"All creatures of the air recognize natural leadership," he replied with his usual modesty, totally forgetting the resistance he met in Vancouver.

Manning Park was beautiful. Outside the cities, tall trees, clean air, mountain vistas made me want to take deep breaths and forget about murder investigations. The hotel sat nestled among the pines like it belonged there, which I supposed it did after however many decades.

"There's Helena," D said, pointing to a woman standing near the entrance.

She looked different than she had in Vancouver. Less commanding, more worried. Her emotions were a swirl of anxiety and determination with undertones of something I couldn't quite identify. Perhaps she was trying to assemble her lies.

D found a parking spot away from the main entrance, and I let Destroyer out of his cage as discreetly as possible.

"I will conduct aerial reconnaissance," he announced, stretching his wings. "These provincial birds will require proper organization."

"Be diplomatic," I warned him. One day he'd run into someone who didn't buy his megalomania and I'd have to jump in and save him. I hoped that wasn't today.

"I am always diplomatic. I simply expect appropriate respect for my obvious superiority." He flew off toward the trees, and I could already hear irritated cawing from the local crow population. At least some things never changed.

"Ms. Fortuna," Helena said, approaching us as we got our bags from the car. "Thank you for coming so quickly."

"What exactly happened?" I asked, not bothering with pleasantries. If there was a dead body involved, we needed to get straight to business. And, frankly, I was done with catering to the Vancouver Council's paranoia and deceit. Maybe if I channeled a little crow confidence I'd grow my own.

"We found Amalia Svoboda in her room this morning," Helena said, glancing around to make sure no plain guests were within earshot. "At first we thought natural causes, but..."

"But it wasn't natural causes," Mark finished before I could say the same.

"Definitely magical. We've managed to convince the hotel staff that she's simply unwell and needs to rest. The stay-away spell will reinforce that message, but we are only booked in for a few more days."

I looked around the parking area and grounds. "How many plain humans are here?"

"A handful of guests, plus the staff. Maybe twenty people total. It's not peak season."

"And the other council members?" If they were all here and the only witches around, then my pool of suspects was small.

"Inside. We had the conference room booked for our brainstorming sessions, so it's a good place to... coordinate our response." She straightened her shoulders and looked at me, ignoring D and Mark. "We expect a fast resolution so we can return to our duties."

That sent a flare of shock from Mark. I guess he wasn't expecting the attitude.

"So by 'coordinate our response' I assume you mean 'argue about what to do.' This will take as long as it takes. I expect your cooperation. First, I need to see the scene and talk to whoever found the body."

The world didn't blow up at my words. In fact, Helena's

emotions flashed a little respect and fear before her shield slammed down. "Of course. But first, let me show you what we've done to contain the situation."

As we walked toward the hotel entrance, I noticed a squirrel watching us from a nearby tree. Unlike the Vancouver squirrel who'd been too busy and important to help, this one seemed curious.

I told the others to go ahead and walked over to the tree. "Excuse me," I said. "Could I ask you something?"

The squirrel's ears perked up. "You can talk to us! That's new. What do you want to know?"

"Have you noticed anything unusual around the hotel recently? Strange people, weird smells, anything out of the ordinary?"

"Oh yes," the squirrel said, scampering down to a lower branch. "Bad magic smell from window in back. Made all of us want to stay away from that side of the building. Not many of us come close in dark time now."

"Bad magic how?" Interesting that he could recognize a scent of magic's purpose. I hoped that wasn't going to be the next level of my emotional power. Although the hexes had smelled like burning rubber when I removed them.

"Like when lightning strikes too close, but... angry. And there was a person walking around in the dark last night. Didn't see who, but they smelled nervous." The squirrel's tail twitched as he spoke.

That was more helpful than anything the Vancouver animals had been willing to share.

"Would you be willing to keep watching and let me know if you notice anything else?"

The squirrel's eyes lit up. "Yes. New things to do! Fun. I will marshal everyone to keep watch for evil doings."

Oh no, had I created another megalomaniac? "What's your name?"

"Nutkin," the squirrel said, surprised I'd thought to ask. "You are a protector. I smell good things around you."

"Yes. My name is Cossi." I thanked him and promised to check in later. At least someone here was enthusiastic about helping. I didn't hold out much optimism that the council would be happy.

Helena had been waiting patiently during my conversation, though I could sense her impatience growing.

"Local intelligence gathering," I explained as we entered the hotel.

The lobby was exactly what you'd expect from a wilderness lodge—lots of wood, comfortable furniture, and rustic charm. The kind of atmosphere that made city people feel like they were roughing it while still having room service. A few guests were scattered around reading or playing cards, looking perfectly normal and unaware that there was a dead body upstairs.

"The concealment spell?" I asked Helena quietly.

"Confusion and redirection," she said. "Anyone who asks about Amalia gets the impression she's resting and doesn't want to be disturbed."

"How long will that hold?" I hoped the witch who cast it was strong enough that we wouldn't be reinforcing it every few hours.

"A few days, maybe. It depends on how often it's triggered."

She didn't need to say more. A dead body was hard to explain away indefinitely, even with magic. "Where are the other council members?"

"Conference room. They're... discussing options." Based

on the stress I could sense from Helena, those discussions weren't going well.

"Before we join them," Mark said, "I need to know what magical protections you've put in place. If this was murder, the killer might still be here."

"Other than warding the room where Amalia was found," Helena said, "we've established a perimeter around the hotel to detect any magical signatures trying to leave the area."

"Who set up the wards?" Mark asked in full detective mode. "I have ones specific to this situation."

"Elizabeth and I worked together on them." She looked him up and down, assessing his importance. "We are fully capable, thank you."

Two people I didn't trust. "If Mark decides they need to be replaced, we will do it. Now, who has access to Amalia's room, not just since her death?"

"Just the council members. We thought it was important to preserve the scene." Helena glanced over at the reception counter where D was checking us in. "We all have access to each other's accommodations."

I appreciated that they'd at least tried to maintain some investigative protocols, even if their cover-up methods were questionable. Unfortunately, the entire pool of suspects had access to the body and places to drop evidence to frame a colleague. Thank goodness we didn't have to rely on finger-prints and DNA.

"All right," I said. "Let's go see what the others have to say, and then I want to examine the body."

As we headed toward the conference room, I caught a glimpse of Destroyer through one of the windows. He was perched on a branch surrounded by what looked like a very animated discussion with several local crows. At least someone was having a productive day.

D ran up to join us before we opened the door. Handing Mark and me each a key card, he said, "I dropped off our bags."

The conference room was smaller than the one in Vancouver, but it was packed with tense witches. Elizabeth Morrison looked up as we entered, and I could immediately sense the mix of relief and apprehension from the group. No helpful aura of guilt, but it had to be here.

"Ms. Fortuna, thank goodness," Elizabeth said. "We need to resolve this quickly. We have business to return to, and that includes recruiting a new member."

"Tell me what happened," I said, taking a seat at the table. "Everything, from the beginning."

15

The story the council told me was straightforward enough, though I was starting to assume that everything this group said needed to be taken with a generous helping of salt.

According to Elizabeth, they'd come to Manning Park for a retreat to discuss how to better handle situations like the one with Marcus. The irony wasn't lost on me—they'd decided to brainstorm about community management after I'd solved their problem in a way they hadn't liked.

"We arrived yesterday afternoon," Maria Santos said, her silver hair even more severely pulled back than usual. "Seven of us, including Beatrix Dai, our intelligence officer."

Intelligence officer? I didn't know councils had those. "Where is Ms. Dai now?"

"She left early this morning to investigate the source of the tea," Helena said. "None of us have the magical expertise to determine if it was tampered with before it reached the hotel."

I made a mental note to talk to this Beatrix person when

she returned. How many other council roles were there that I had no clue about?

"We had dinner together, discussed some preliminary ideas, and retired to our rooms around ten PM," Elizabeth continued. "This morning, when Amalia didn't come down for breakfast, Helena went to check on her."

"I knocked first," Helena said. "When she didn't answer, I used a simple unlocking spell. The door wasn't warded or anything. I found her sitting in the chair by the window, looking like she'd just... stopped."

"No signs of struggle?" Mark asked.

"None. But there was definitely residual magic in the room. Dark magic."

I could feel the emotions around the table shifting as they talked about finding Amalia's body. Fear, certainly, but also something that felt like... calculation? Someone was working very hard to present the right emotional response.

"Who was Amalia rooming near?" I asked. If I looked too closely, I'd get distracted from what we came to do. I had no confidence in my ability to dive deep and find the killer through emotions.

"We have rooms along the same corridor," Robert Kim said. "I was next door, Helena was across the hall."

"And the others?"

"James and Ormand are at the other end of the hall," Maria said. "I have the room between them and the others. Beatrix is across from me."

So everyone had been close enough to visit Amalia without being seen by other guests. Perfect.

"What were you hoping to accomplish at this retreat?" D asked, looking up from his notes. "You said you were discussing new approaches."

That question produced an interesting spike of tension

around the table. I kept it to myself. "And me," Destroyer whispered. No need for the lower volume—he wasn't in the room.

"We wanted to develop better protocols," Elizabeth said after a pause. "More efficient ways to handle situations like the one with the Reeves family."

"You mean ways to avoid calling in a protector?" I asked. Their goal of efficiency didn't leave much room for understanding and empathy.

"Ways to resolve issues before they require outside intervention," Maria said, and I caught a hint of resentment in her tone.

Ah. So this retreat was about figuring out how to manage their community without having to admit they needed help. I guess I'd underestimated how much they resented my decision to give the family haven.

"Did Amalia agree with those goals?" Mark asked.

Another pause, longer this time. "Amalia had... different ideas about community management," Helena said carefully.

"Different how?" he pressed.

"She thought we should be more collaborative," James O'Brien said, speaking up for the first time. "More willing to work with outside communities and authorities."

"Like protectors," I said. Were there other authorities?

"Among others," James said.

Should I push on this? I decided to wait and not display my lack of knowledge. We had enough to digest anyway. A potential motive—disagreement about how the community should operate. The question was whether anyone had been angry enough about those disagreements to kill Amalia.

"I need to see the body now," I said, standing up. "Mark,

D, you're with me. The rest of you... please stay here and available."

"Ms. Fortuna," Elizabeth said, "surely you don't suspect one of us?"

"I suspect everyone until I have reason not to," I said. Did she think a plain human could have poisoned Amalia? Or was Manning Park filled with witches and shifters? "That's how investigations work."

The emotions around the table spiked again—more fear, more anger, and definitely more calculation from someone who was working very hard to look innocent.

How had they missed the facts? They were the only people around who could have used magic at all. Unless they were thinking someone set up the poison beforehand and that could have been a plain human. The tea wasn't spelled, but surely Amalia would have sensed the danger. Someone used magic to hide the deadly ingredients. But premeditation was an interesting idea and opened up the suspect pool way too far. Perhaps this mysterious Beatrix was following up on that by looking for the source of the tea.

16

As we headed for the residential side of the building, I tried to organize what I knew. A council member dead under mysterious circumstances, disagreements about community policy, and a group of witches who had already proven themselves willing to lie to a protector when it suited their purposes.

"What do you think?" D asked quietly as we walked.

"I think this retreat was about more than brainstorming," I said. "And I think someone decided Amalia's different ideas about collaboration were a problem that needed to be solved permanently. Someone who had no intention of changing the rules. Getting rid of the most vocal opposition would allow them to move on."

"Any guesses about who?" Mark asked. "I mean, we already know the council oaths can be manipulated. Otherwise we would never think of these people as suspects."

I couldn't imagine another Phillip in this group of people. But maybe stealing emotions wasn't the only way to circumvent the protections. "Too early to tell. But someone down there is doing a very good job of hiding their emotions, which means they've had practice at deception."

Mark pulled out a pair of gloves as we approached Amalia's room. "Just in case the spells activate by contact."

Helena had given us the key to the room, and I could feel the wards as we reached the door. They were strong, but they felt... incomplete somehow. Like they were designed to keep things in rather than keep people out.

"Ready?" Mark asked.

I nodded, though I wasn't sure anyone could ever be ready to see a murdered council member.

He opened the door, and we stepped into what had been Amalia Svoboda's last room.

The first thing that hit me was the smell—not decay, thankfully, but the lingering scent of magic gone wrong. It reminded me of burning electronics mixed with something organic and unpleasant. Not quite like the hexes, but still more than unpleasant.

Amalia was sitting in a chair by the window, just as Helena had described. At first glance, she looked like she might be sleeping, but there was something profoundly wrong about the stillness of her body.

"No obvious trauma," Mark observed, walking carefully around the chair.

"But look at her expression," D said, waving me around to the front.

I moved closer and saw what he meant. Amalia's face was frozen in an expression of complete surprise, like she'd been interrupted in the middle of a conversation by something totally unexpected.

"She knew her killer," I said. "This wasn't a random attack or a break-in. She was talking to someone she trusted, and then..."

"Then they killed her," Mark finished.

I reached out with my emotion-reading ability, trying to sense any residual feelings in the room. What I found made my skin crawl.

"There was betrayal here," I said. "And satisfaction. Whoever did this felt very happy with the result."

That narrowed down my suspect list considerably. Killing someone in anger was one thing. Killing someone and feeling satisfied about it suggested a much more calculated mind. Now I just had to find that person.

"Any physical evidence?" I asked Mark.

"I'll need more time to process the scene properly, but..." He pointed to the nightstand. "Look at this."

On the small table beside the bed was a teacup, still half full of what looked like chamomile tea.

"She was having tea with someone," D said. "At least that's not a lie."

"Or someone gave her tea," I corrected. "Or left it here to support the story. Either way, it suggests this was a social visit that turned deadly."

"Can you test it?" Mark asked. "I mean, Mrs. V can, but I've never known if it was a protector thing, or if she just knew everything."

"I can try a small magical analysis," I said, thinking back to a few lessons. "I'm not sure if we can rely on what I find."

As I moved closer to examine the teacup, I heard Destroyer's voice in my mind.

"The forest birds have been moderately helpful," he said. "They observed a witch leaving this building around midnight, but they could not identify which witch due to inadequate lighting. I believe the truth is more like they aren't observant enough."

"Male or female?" I asked silently. Destroyer's news supported Nutkin's report, so it felt like progress.

"Again, they did not observe, or perhaps they have not trained their minds to remember. I will add that to my list of training."

If he was starting a boot camp, I would have to step in and hope I had influence over emperors.

"We need to interview everyone again," I said to Mark and D, passing on Destroyer's report. "Separately this time, and more thoroughly. Someone in that conference room is lying about what happened last night. I need to contact this Beatrix, too."

"Agreed," Mark said. "But first, let's see what else this room can tell us."

As we continued examining the scene, I tried to push down the growing certainty that this case was going to be more complicated than anything I'd dealt with before. And somewhere in the hotel below us, a killer was probably wondering how much the protector actually knew about murder investigations.

17

A fter we finished examining Amalia's room, I stood in the hallway trying to figure out what to do next. I'd solved murders before, but those had been on Henbane where everyone wanted to help. Here, I had a feeling people were going to be more interested in protecting themselves than finding the truth.

"We should probably split them up," I said to Mark and D, hoping I sounded more confident than I felt. "Harder for them to coordinate their stories if they're not all sitting together. And easier for me to identify individual emotions."

"Good thinking," Mark said. "Even if they've come up with a common story, questions can sort out lies. It works on teenage witches and adults who've gotten too far in a spat. Who do you want to start with?"

I tried to remember the emotions I'd sensed in the conference room. Elizabeth had been controlled, Helena anxious. But what did that actually tell me about who might be a killer? For all I knew, I was completely misreading everything.

"Helena, I guess," I said. "She found the body, so maybe

she noticed something the others didn't. And she's been our contact, so we've had the most contact with her."

"Do not trust anyone," Destroyer said.

"Do you read trust in my thoughts?" I appreciated his help, but he was way off.

"Not yet, but do not be influenced."

When we returned to the conference room, I could feel the tension spike as soon as we walked in. Everyone was trying very hard to look innocent, which just made them all seem more suspicious.

"Helena," I said, "could I speak with you privately? Is there somewhere we can talk?"

"There's a smaller meeting room down the hall," she said, standing up quickly. She wasn't eager to join me— more like wanting to get this over with.

"The rest of you, please stay here," Mark said with the authority of his police power to shut down any resistance. "We'll be speaking with each of you individually."

The smaller meeting room had windows overlooking the forest, which would have been peaceful if I wasn't about to interrogate someone about murder. Helena sat across from me and Mark at the small table, and I could sense her nervousness ramping up. She must have assumed I'd be alone.

"This is just to help me sort out what I know," I said, though I wasn't entirely sure she believed me. "I need to understand what happened from your perspective."

"Of course," Helena said, folding her hands in front of her. "I want to help however I can."

Yeah, sure. It was like she didn't know I could read her. "Tell me about last night. After dinner, what did you do?"

"We continued our discussions in the conference room about the issues we'd come here to resolve."

I was working on too many assumptions about that. "What issues specifically?"

Helena hesitated, and I caught a flicker of embarrassment. "Amalia had... concerns about how some of us handled the situation with the Reeves family. She thought this retreat would be a good opportunity to discuss better approaches."

"Better than what?" Mark asked.

"Better than my approach, specifically." Helena's emotions shifted to guilt and defensiveness. "She thought I'd been too aggressive, too focused on control rather than collaboration. I was working with Maria, but Amalia seemed to think it was all my idea."

"So this retreat was partly about Amalia wanting to address your methods?" Like some kind of performance review?

"Not just mine. No witch can control the council."

That painted the retreat in a different light. Not just a discussion, but an attempt to close a rift?

"I told you not to be influenced. Humans are too controlled by jealousy and resentment," Destroyer said. I couldn't deny he was right, and I didn't want to ask how he knew.

I tried to ignore him and focus on Helena's emotional state. Definitely embarrassed and defensive, but not murderous. At least, I didn't think so. How was I supposed to tell the difference? "What time did your discussion end?"

"Around nine-thirty, I think. Everyone went to their rooms after that." She gained control of her emotional shield and her reactions became muted.

"What did you do then?" Mark asked. I liked how he kept her off-kilter by jumping in with questions.

She shrugged like it wasn't important. "Read for a while,

then went to sleep. Nothing unusual. I didn't go kill my fellow council member."

Did she think we'd just take her word for it? I glanced at Mark to see if he noticed a lie, but he kept his eyes on Helena. I changed tack. "Did you hear anything unusual during the night?"

Helena paused, and I caught another flicker of uncertainty. "I thought I heard a door close around midnight, but I was half asleep. It could have been anyone. A plain human guest, a staff member—I didn't go looking."

"Any voices? Footsteps in the hallway?" Mark asked.

"No, just the door." The look she gave him undercut her words, but I didn't know why. "It wasn't loud enough to fully wake me up."

That matched what Destroyer's birds had reported, which was either a good sign for my investigation or a coincidence.

"When you found Amalia this morning, what exactly did you see?" I asked.

"As I said, she was sitting in the chair by the window. At first I thought she was just... I don't know, enjoying the view or something. But when I called her name and she didn't respond..." Helena shuddered. "I knew something was wrong."

"What time was this?" Mark asked.

"Around eight. I'd expected her at breakfast by seven-thirty."

Interesting that they'd waited a half hour before checking on her when the purpose of the conference needed everyone's point of view. "Did you notice the teacup then?"

"Yes. I wondered why she'd been having tea in her room instead of coming down for breakfast."

That made more sense than late-night tea drinking. "Did you touch anything in the room?"

Helena closed her eyes at the memory and her emotions flooded with sadness. "Just to check if she was... to make sure she was really gone. Then I went to get Elizabeth."

"Did you notice if the door to her room was locked when you first tried it?" Mark asked.

"No, it opened right away. That's part of why I was worried—Amalia always locked her door. We all do. It wouldn't help anyone to have housekeeping drop by and see evidence of magic."

I studied Helena's emotions as she talked. Anxiety, sadness, guilt about the professional conflict, but nothing that screamed murderer. Of course, I had no idea what murderer emotions actually looked like, so maybe I was missing something obvious. "Helena, how serious was Amalia's concern about your methods? Was your position on the council in jeopardy?"

Her emotional response spiked—definitely guilt and fear. "She hadn't made any formal complaints yet. But yes, I was worried about what might happen if she convinced the others that I was... unsuitable for council work. Or if they simply allowed me to be the scapegoat."

So Helena had a motive. But lots of people had workplace conflicts without resorting to murder, right?

"Ask her about magical abilities," Destroyer advised. "Can she cast the type of spell that killed the victim?"

That was actually a good question. One I could answer by checking on her powers somewhere. If D couldn't find the information, then I'd ask later. "Thank you," I said. "Could you ask Elizabeth to come in?"

Helena left, and I sat trying to figure out if I'd learned

anything useful. Mark and D muttered as they updated the investigation log.

"You are overthinking," Destroyer said. "Interview the leader next and compare their stories for inconsistencies."

"I'm not overthinking, I'm thinking. There's a difference."

"I disagree, but if you will not take my advice, I have emperor business."

A few minutes later Elizabeth Morrison entered the room. Where Helena had been nervous, Elizabeth was controlled. Her emotions were carefully shielded, and she sat down with composed confidence—she expected to be in charge.

"I hope Helena was helpful," she said, taking a seat without being asked. Yes, she was going to try to control the interview.

I had a different expectation. "Very helpful. Now I'd like to hear your perspective on last night."

"Certainly. We had dinner, continued our discussions until around nine-thirty, then everyone retired. I read some reports until about eleven, then went to sleep. I didn't hear anything unusual."

Her story matched Helena's timeline, which was either good or evidence they'd coordinated their answers. There was a lot of detail missing, which was what I wanted to help sift out the killer from the just extremely annoying members of the council.

"What was the focus of your evening discussion?" Mark asked.

"Developing better protocols for community management. We all recognized the need for improvement after the situation with the Reeves family." She waved her hand in dismissal. I'm not sure if it was at the original problem, or that family specifically, or at what she saw as any problem that got in her way.

I let it go and said, "Helena mentioned that Amalia had specific concerns about how that situation was handled."

Elizabeth's emotional control slipped slightly—a flash of irritation before she composed herself again. "Amalia felt some of our methods were too... direct. She preferred a more collaborative approach."

"With outside authorities? Like protectors?" D asked. He didn't look up from his keyboard, but Elizabeth radiated surprise that he'd spoken.

"Among others, yes."

I could sense Elizabeth's resentment about that, even through her emotional shields. "Did you agree with Amalia's assessment?"

"I believe communities function best when they maintain independence and resolve problems internally." She plucked a tiny piece of lint from the arm of her chair.

"Why are you letting her lie to you?" Destroyer asked.

"I thought you were off doing emperor stuff." I didn't need the distraction.

"I am able to do multiple tasks," he said. "I will leave you to your own mistakes."

I turned my attention back to the room. "Were there heated disagreements during your discussion?"

That question surprised her too. Elizabeth blinked and hesitated. Her shield was back in place before I could figure out why.

"Nothing beyond normal professional discourse," she said. "When you are exploring change, people get... afraid of losing their influence."

Mark jumped in again. "When you warded Amalia's

room this morning, did you notice anything specific about the magical residue?"

This got her attention. "Yes. Dark magic. Probably something designed to interfere with life force."

"How long would a spell like that take to cast?" Mark asked. "Are we talking about something quick, or would the killer have needed time to prepare?"

"Difficult to say without knowing the exact method. But most life force spells require concentration and intent. Not something you could do casually."

I followed the path this question raised. "Are any of the council members familiar with that type of magic?"

Elizabeth's body relaxed with the change of direction. "Theoretically, perhaps. It's not something we would study practically."

The way she said it made me wonder if theoretical knowledge was enough. Mrs. V had always said magic was more about intent than technique. "Is there anyone else who might have had access to the hotel last night?"

"Not that we're aware of. We chose this location for its isolation. This is the off-season for Manning Park."

I couldn't understand why she didn't make the logical connection. Everything pointed to a council member as the killer. "Thank you," I said. "I may have more questions later."

After Elizabeth left, I sat staring out at the forest, trying to make sense of what I'd learned. Mark was working with D to keep our records updated. I wondered when we'd have time to review it all.

"What do you think?" I asked both of them.

"Both had motives," Mark said. "Helena faced professional consequences, Elizabeth resented Amalia's approach. But neither of them felt like killers to me."

"Any big lies?" Everyone told little ones all the time.

"I guess we won't know until they have to say whether they killed her or not." D smiled when he said it. "We can't just do that, right? We need to know more about them to know if they can lie the way Phillip did."

"If only it were that easy," Mark said. "Both of them were hiding something, but the lies were all small. And yes, D is right. Before we knew what Phillip did, I'd say just ask. But now we know people can cover their true selves too easily."

18

The next three interviews were like watching variations on the same theme—everyone had the same basic story, everyone had reasonable alibis, and everyone seemed to have some issue with Amalia's collaborative approach to community management.

Robert Kim was nervous and kept fidgeting with his cufflinks. He'd been in his room reading financial reports until late, heard nothing unusual, and thought Amalia's ideas about working with outside authorities were "impractical for maintaining community security." When Mark asked him about his magical abilities, Robert admitted he was "more of an administrator than a practitioner," which seemed like a diplomatic way of saying his magic wasn't strong enough to kill anyone.

James O'Brien was more forthcoming about the tensions in the group. He confirmed that the retreat had been partly about addressing Amalia's concerns with how certain council members handled community issues, but he insisted the discussions had been "professional, not personal." His room was at the end of the hall, and he'd heard nothing during the night except "maybe some plumbing noises around midnight." He seemed genuinely sad about Amalia's death, but Mark noted that he also seemed relieved that the confrontation between her and Helena wouldn't happen now.

Ormand Mistry was the most controlled of the three, answering questions with precision. He described the evening's discussion as "productive disagreement about strategic direction" and said he'd gone to bed early because he had "important calls to make this morning." When I asked about his relationship with Amalia, he said they'd "maintained professional respect despite philosophical differences."

Maria Santos didn't add much more than confirm she heard someone walking around late at night. She hadn't checked the time, but it was late.

"Why do none of these witches mourn her?" Destroyer asked as we finished with Ormand. "Are they less than crows? When one of my flock dies, we feel loss."

He had a point. Everyone seemed more concerned about the inconvenience of a murder investigation than the actual murder.

"Hope it is because they are waiting to learn who killed her. Humans are good at prioritizing."

"Grief does not wait on convenience. This is a clue and I have pointed you in the right direction."

"Thank you, O Mighty Emperor." I let him mutter on for a few minutes about respect and then he stopped.

I passed on his thought because he might not have solved the case, but he had pointed out something we hadn't noticed.

"I don't think they liked her," D said. "And so far no one has actually said they agreed with her."

By the time we'd finished all the interviews, it was late afternoon and I was more confused than when we'd started. Everyone had alibis, everyone had motives, and everyone was being just honest enough to seem credible while holding back just enough to seem suspicious.

"So what now?" D asked as the three of us gathered in the smaller meeting room.

"Now I have to make sure no one leaves," I said, trying to sound more confident than I felt. "If the killer is one of the council members, I can't let them go back to Vancouver before we figure out who it is."

"How are you going to enforce that?" Mark asked. "You can't exactly arrest them."

"I can't, but I can bind them with their own council oath."

"Remember what Phillip did after swearing the oath," Mark said. "Can you make sure they aren't borrowing emotions so the words mean nothing?"

I hadn't noticed Phillip's lack of real emotion, so the answer was no. "It must be rare, right? And I'll be careful to word it right. No room to interpret it in a way that would allow someone to run to Vancouver."

"Well, the protector's authority should have some effect, right?" I wished I believed that without having to remind myself all the time.

We returned to the main conference room, where the council members were sitting around looking uncomfortable and checking their phones. Elizabeth looked up as we entered. "Ms. Fortuna, have you learned anything useful from the interviews?"

"I've learned that someone with strong magic killed Amalia Svoboda," I said, trying to channel Mrs. V's no-nonsense tone. "There are no other witches or shifters around, right? What I haven't learned yet is which one of you did such an awful thing."

The emotional response around the table was immediate—spikes of fear, anger, and what felt like guilt from multiple directions.

"Surely you don't seriously suspect—" Robert started.

"I seriously suspect everyone," I said, cutting him off. "Which is why no one is leaving this hotel until we resolve this."

"You can't keep us here," Ormand said. "We have businesses to run, responsibilities—"

"You have a responsibility to your murdered colleague," Mark said firmly. "And to the community you're supposed to serve."

"Besides," I added, "you're all bound by your council oath to follow protector orders during community crises. I'd say murder qualifies."

Helena looked surprised. "You're invoking the council oath?"

"I am." I hoped I sounded more certain about this than I felt as I activated the oath. Although I was starting to feel less like I was faking it. "You all feel the pull of your oath?" Every head around the table nodded. I'd given thought to the words. I said them fast to avoid chickening out. "No one in this room will leave the area of the lodge without my permission."

The room went very quiet. I could feel them weighing their options, testing the magical compulsion that came with oath-binding.

"This is highly irregular," Elizabeth said, but there was resignation in her tone.

"Murder is highly irregular," I replied. "Staying here for a few more days while we find Amalia's killer is the least irregular thing we can do about it."

"What about our obligations in Vancouver?" James asked.

"You all have devices, so handle business and council matters remotely," I said, making an executive decision. "Everything else can wait. It's not going to take long."

"I most certainly cannot—" Helena started.

"Yes, you can," I said, and this time I did let a little of my protector authority slip into my voice. "Unless you think council politics are more important than finding out who murdered Amalia."

The magical compulsion settled over the room like a weight. I could see the moment each of them realized they literally couldn't leave—not without breaking an oath that was bound into their magical cores.

"Well," Ormand said dryly, "I suppose we're having an extended retreat."

"How long do you expect this to take?" Robert asked, pulling out his phone to presumably cancel appointments.

"As long as it takes," I said. "But I suggest everyone cooperate fully, because the sooner we catch the killer, the sooner you can all go home."

"And if we don't find the killer?" Helena asked.

I hadn't thought that far ahead, which was probably something I should have considered before binding them all here.

"We will," I said, hoping I sounded more confident than I felt. "We have to."

"I am proud of you," Destroyer said. "Now you are acting like a familiar worthy of an emperor."

I thanked him for the vote of confidence.

As the council members reluctantly began making phone calls to rearrange their schedules, I caught Mark's eye. He looked impressed, which was nice, but also slightly concerned.

"Beatrix Dai," he said quietly. "She's still out there."

"She won't be bound by the oath," D said. "She was here when the murder happened."

"I need Ms. Dai's contact information," I said to the entire council. "I want her to return here."

"I'll call her back," Maria said. "She's not far."

I watched as she sent the text and received a thumbs-up emoji in reply.

19

I woke up the next morning feeling like my brain had been stuffed with cotton. Too much information, too many suspects, and absolutely no clear direction forward. The council members were all being cooperative now that they were magically bound to stay, but cooperative didn't necessarily mean helpful.

"Do not linger in self-pity," Destroyer announced. He was perched on a branch outside my window. I guess I should be happy that he didn't have the ability to wake me up.

"It's confusion. I'm surprised your supreme powers can't tell the difference," I said, heading for the bathroom to get myself ready.

"Perhaps the lack is in you," he said with a sniff. "I will continue to search for clues."

It was so early that I figured Mark was still asleep in the next room. D had stayed up late working on some kind of timeline analysis that involved a lot of charts and colored pens, so he probably needed a long sleep-in. I pulled on my jacket and headed outside, hoping a walk in the fresh air might help me think more clearly.

Manning Park in the early morning was beautiful—pine trees stretching toward a sky that was just starting to lighten, hushed enough to remind me there was a world outside of murder investigations and council politics.

I found a trail that led away from the hotel and started walking, letting my mind wander. Maybe if I stopped trying so hard to solve everything, the answer would come to me. Mom always said that sometimes the best way to find something was to stop looking for it.

"Excuse me," I called out to a chipmunk I spotted near a fallen log. "Could I ask you something?"

The chipmunk froze, then slowly turned to look at me cautiously, poised to run if I made the wrong move. "You are Nutkin's witch?" he asked in a surprisingly low voice. Perhaps Alvin and the Chipmunks wasn't a good reference for animal speech.

"Yes, that's me. I'm investigating something that happened at the hotel, and I wondered if you'd noticed anything unusual recently."

"We don't go near that place," the chipmunk said immediately. "Not safe. All humans are unusual."

"Not safe how?" I thought Manning Park would be perfectly secure for all kinds of animals.

"Humans with guns came once. Supposed to be no killing here, just pictures, but they killed lots of us. Now we stay away." He flicked a glance at the nearest tree but didn't move otherwise.

That explained why I couldn't find a lot of animals around the lodge. I remembered Nutkin's enthusiasm about being a woodland detective—he probably didn't know about the hunting incident, or he wasn't alive when it happened. "When did the hunters shoot you?"

"Last year. Since then, we watch from far away but don't get close."

Maybe some animals were willing to take more risks than others. "Have you seen anything unusual from your distant watching?"

The chipmunk considered this. "Someone walking around in the dark. Night before last, maybe? Didn't go near to see who."

Too many reports of this person to doubt they existed. "Walking where?"

"Around the building. Back and forth, like they were thinking hard about something."

Someone pacing outside the hotel the night Amalia died. That was potentially useful, except it could have been anyone—a guest who couldn't sleep, a council member getting fresh air, or the killer working up nerve for murder. "Did you see what they looked like?"

"Too dark, too far away. Just someone walking."

I thanked the chipmunk and continued down the trail, hoping I might find other animals who'd observed something more specific.

A few minutes later, I spotted a family of raccoons near a stream. Raccoons were usually curious, intelligent, and observant. The ones on Henbane were able to bring me evidence. "Good morning," I said. "It's a good day for foraging." I had to get better at small talk.

The largest raccoon, probably the father, looked up from washing something in the stream. "You're the one who talks to animals," he said. "Bird said you might come."

"Destroyer?" He'd love being called "bird," not "emperor."

"Crazy crow? Wants us to be his army?"

"That's him." I tried not to smile at the description. "What did you notice about the hotel?"

"We don't go close," he said, echoing the chipmunk. "Humans don't keep promises."

"The hunters?"

"Killed three cousins. Two deer right after. Didn't take food, just liked killing."

The anger in his voice was clear, and I couldn't blame him. No wonder the local animals avoided the lodge. "But you watch from a distance?"

"Sometimes. Two dark times ago, someone was walking around outside the building. Middle of the night."

Another report of the same thing. We'd have to figure out how to identify this mystery person. "Anything else unusual?"

"Loud voices earlier that night. Coming from the building. Don't understand words, but someone was angry."

That was new information. Loud, angry voices suggested the evening discussion hadn't been as professionally calm as the council members had claimed. "What time was this?"

"Don't know time like humans. After dark, before darkest."

So sometime between the end of their nine-thirty discussion and midnight when someone was seen leaving. The timeline was getting more interesting.

I talked to a few more animals as I walked—a pair of squirrels, a deer who'd been drinking from the stream, and even a porcupine who was remarkably chatty for something covered in quills. They all told variations of the same story: they stayed away from the hotel because of the hunters, but they'd noticed someone walking around outside the night before last.

"You should have asked me—no one saw anything useful," Destroyer observed when I paused by a clearing to think. "I am their emperor, I will gather their stories."

I remembered the "crazy crow" comment. Unfortunately, Destroyer reads my thoughts. "Raccoons are not respectful." He managed to inject scorn into his tone rather than the usual superiority.

I wasn't going to jump on the subject of his ability to reign over all the animals. "They lack trust in humans," I said. "Which is understandable given what happened with the hunters. The animals can't gather intel if they are afraid to come close."

The walk wasn't wasted. I had confirmation that someone had been walking around outside the night Amalia died from multiple sources, and that there had been loud, angry voices coming from the building earlier that evening. But I still didn't know if the person walking around was the killer, someone who couldn't sleep, or just someone getting fresh air after a tense discussion.

The frustrating thing was that every piece of information seemed to raise more questions instead of providing answers.

———————

20

On my way back from talking to the animals, I realized I'd been so focused on magical suspects that I'd barely thought about the mundane guests and staff. If the concealment spells were working properly, they shouldn't have noticed anything unusual, but it seemed like good investigative practice to check. If anyone suspected there was more than a slight illness, we would lose our advantage.

"Don't rely on the traitorous council," Destroyer said. "Replace their spell with your own."

"I will if we need to," I said. "I really hope we'll solve this today."

I found a few guests in the lobby area—a middle-aged couple reading newspapers and a man with hiking gear who looked like he was planning to hit the trails. The hiker looked approachable, so I wandered over to where he was studying a trail map.

"Planning a good hike?" I asked.

"Hoping to," he said with a friendly smile. "I'm Rufus Walker. You're staying here too?"

"For a few days, yes. I'm Cossi. This is a great place for our conference," I said, hoping to keep the cover story going. "So remote and easy to relax."

"Oh yes, very quiet. Perfect for getting away from the city noise." Rufus folded his map and tucked it into his jacket pocket. "Well, mostly quiet. Someone was up walking around pretty late night before last, but I figured they just couldn't sleep. Happens to me sometimes when I'm somewhere new."

I shouldn't feel shocked. None of the witches would waste energy hiding such a normal activity. "Walking around where?"

"Outside, I think. I heard footsteps on the gravel. Went on for a while—back and forth, like someone was pacing. But hey, people deal with insomnia differently."

Constant confirmation of the same thing was useful, I guess. What would be better were new details. I chatted with Rufus for a few more minutes about hiking trails and local wildlife, trying not to seem like I was probing for information when I was. I said goodbye and headed to the front desk where I found a young woman who looked like she'd been working here for a while.

"Hi there," I said. "I'm Cossi, I'm here with the business group. How are things going?"

"I'm Toni," she said with a professional smile. "Everything's been fine. It's a bit of a slow period. Mostly people come in the summer for hiking and the winter for cross-country skiing. Right now, it's conferences, like your group, or stops along the way to somewhere else. It's kind of my favorite time of year."

"I'm just checking to make sure we're not disturbing your other guests. We tend to forget the time when we're deep in problem-solving mode." Fingers crossed that she'd give me the name of the mystery walker.

"No complaints," Toni said with a shrug. "We only have a few people on at night. One of the security staff makes patrols. No report of incidents."

It didn't mean anything. The timing of a security check and the pacing of the clearly stressed person wouldn't necessarily have come together. And pacing around was very different from checking the perimeter. "What kind of incidents?"

"Once we had a mother bear and cubs in the trees around the back. It could have been a problem, but we were able to warn people. Nothing more than that."

"Good to know," I said. "Are we the only large group staying here right now?"

"Yes, we don't have room to accommodate more than one conference. I hope your friend is feeling better."

I didn't need to check the spell. If it was fading, Toni would be the first to know. "She'll be fine, thanks for asking. Is this all the guests? It seems busy enough."

"People are only here for a night or two, so there's not much to do. And the guest in the cabin put his do-not-disturb sign out the day he arrived."

Cabins? "I didn't realize there were cabins." I used a little power to keep her talking because I suspected she'd realize soon that she shouldn't be sharing so much information.

"Just three of them, back in the trees. Usually used by guests who want extra privacy or are staying longer term. This guest has been here for over a week."

That was interesting. Another guest I didn't know about, staying in a cabin away from the main hotel. Someone who might have seen or heard something useful. A suspect or another plain human?

"I might head over there on my next walk," I said. "A cozy cabin might be fun for a weekend with friends."

As I headed back toward our rooms, I thought about what I'd learned. The concealment spells were working perfectly, and everyone was interpreting the council's behavior as normal business retreat stress. But there was someone else staying on the property that I didn't know about, someone who'd been here longer than the council and might have observed things from a different perspective.

"So hiding the body of this witch has been successful," Destroyer observed.

I glanced around to see if he'd snuck into the lobby. No sign of him. "Very successful. But there's another guest staying in a cabin that I didn't know about."

"The killer?" Destroyer announced more than asked.

"Well, at least a potential suspect or witness," I said. "Someone who's been here long enough to observe the council's routines and plan something. Or maybe saw who was walking around last night—or is our walker."

21

B reakfast at the hotel was a surprisingly normal affair, considering we were sharing the dining room with a murderer. The council members sat at one large table, making polite conversation about weather and hiking trails like they were actually on a business retreat. The mundane guests scattered around the room seemed completely oblivious to the tension that was practically crackling in the air.

Mark, D, and I claimed a corner table where we could talk quietly without being overheard.

"So," Mark said, spreading jam on his toast, "what do we actually know?"

"That I have no idea what I'm doing," I said, poking at my eggs. "Everyone has alibis, everyone has motives, and I can't tell if I'm reading their emotions correctly or just seeing what I expect to see."

"You're not imagining things," D said firmly. "I've been watching them too, and there's definitely something off about the group dynamics."

"Like what?"

"Like the way Maria Santos keeps looking at everyone else like she's calculating something. And how Elizabeth gets tense whenever anyone mentions Amalia's alternative approach. And come to think of it, why are they still discussing the problem? Wouldn't her death end the conflict?"

I nodded, feeling slightly better that D had noticed the same things. "I think it wasn't Amalia against the rest of the council. She had allies, and for now, they want to keep a low profile."

"I don't know if that's good or bad," Mark said. "You think they're afraid of being killed?"

I thought that one over. It didn't feel right somehow. "No. In the best case, they are regrouping and waiting to see if the protector fixes the problem. In the worst case... I don't know."

"Politics are a pain," D said. "We have them on Henbane, but not to this extent. I'll be glad to get home."

I agreed, but politics were always going to be part of my job. "What really bothers me is something from our first meeting with the council. Back in Vancouver, when we were discussing the Reeves situation."

"What about it?" Mark asked.

I dug around in my mind for the right words. Mark wasn't there at the meeting, so I needed to be clear in my explanation. "Maria's emotions were... strange. When we talked about Marcus and his family, she had this spike of something that felt like fear mixed with anger. At the time I thought it was just stress about community exposure, but now..."

"Now you think it might have been something more personal?" D said. "Or am I missing something?"

"Maybe. And Amalia was pushing back against the idea

of sending Marcus to that awful place and separating the family, even before I suggested bringing them to Henbane. She didn't actually say it, but I read her emotions."

Mark leaned back in his chair, thinking. "So you're wondering if there was a deeper conflict between Maria and Amalia, not just about how to handle training kids with erratic powers?"

"It's possible. But I could be completely wrong. Maybe Maria was just having a bad day, or maybe I'm remembering her emotions wrong, or maybe—"

"Cossi," D interrupted gently, "stop second-guessing yourself. Your emotion reading has been pretty accurate so far."

I should believe that, but that little voice inside me was having fun undercutting everything I did. "Has it? How can I tell?"

"I watched you in the interviews," he said. "Mark agrees with me. You asked questions we wouldn't have thought of because you knew something."

"I knew there were a lot of lies," Mark said. "But I can't tell if the lie is important. You aren't as easily fooled. You could have pressed harder, but it was too soon. There's a point where you have to let people stew on it."

That was true, but it didn't make me feel much more confident about my abilities. The council had set shields against my power pretty fast.

"Besides," D continued, "even if Maria did have strong feelings about the Reeves situation, that doesn't necessarily make her a killer. She looks like she's in her seventies, so she's at least a hundred. With age comes patience and wisdom. Most older witches I know are more interested in mentoring than murdering."

"We don't know what that does to a witch on the mainland," Mark said. "Age can reinforce all kinds of petty resentments and fears."

"Or power," Destroyer chipped in. "Phillip wanted it."

I refused to point out his own hypocrisy. "Destroyer thinks older witches prefer politics to violence," I said, paraphrasing, then paused as something occurred to me. "But what if that's exactly the point?"

"What do you mean?" D asked, picking up his coffee.

"Let's say Maria is the killer—I'm not willing to ignore the others, but just for a minute. What if she wasn't planning to kill Amalia? What if she was planning something else—like discrediting her politically—and the murder was a mistake or an accident?"

Mark looked interested. "You mean she might have been trying to use magic to manipulate Amalia's thinking, and something went wrong?"

"It's possible. Magic can be unpredictable, especially if you're using spells you're not completely familiar with." I thought for a moment about that statement. That was my experience, but I'm not a witch with a hundred years of experience. "There can't be much magic she hasn't mastered by now, right?"

"Not all witches look beyond their specialty, Cossi. But even if it was an accident, it would still make her the killer," D pointed out. "We don't have the same shades of gray as the plain humans. You kill, you are a murderer."

I wasn't sold on the black-and-white definition, but that was a discussion for another time. "True, but it would change the motive. Instead of planning murder, she might have been planning political sabotage that turned deadly."

I glanced over at the council table, where Maria was calmly discussing hiking trail difficulty levels with Robert Kim. She looked like someone's grandmother, not a killer.

But then again, so had Phillip—well, not a grandmother, but you get the idea—until we discovered he'd been controlling people and committing murder for decades.

"There's another problem with the Maria theory," Mark said quietly.

"What?" I asked, tearing my attention away from the council table.

"The tea," Mark said. "If Maria was trying to manipulate Amalia's thinking, why have tea together? Why not just catch her alone in the hallway or wait for a private moment during their discussions?"

That was a good point. The tea suggested a social visit, someone Amalia trusted enough to invite into her room for a friendly conversation.

"Unless the tea was Maria's idea," I said. "Maybe she suggested they have a private chat to work out their differences, and Amalia agreed because she thought Maria was trying to find a compromise."

"Possible," D said, "but it feels complicated. Why not just vote against Amalia's proposals during council meetings?"

"Because this retreat was specifically about addressing Amalia's concerns with other council members' methods," I said. "If Maria was one of the people Amalia was criticizing, a private conversation might have seemed like the best way to change Amalia's mind before any changes were agreed to."

We sat in silence for a moment, watching the council members finish their breakfast. They all looked so normal, so professional. It was hard to believe one of them had committed murder just two nights ago.

"What about the person walking around outside?" Mark asked. "Do we think that was Maria?"

"Could be anyone," I said. "But if Maria did try to use

magic on Amalia and it went wrong, she might have been pacing around trying to figure out what to do next."

"Or trying to work up the nerve to go back and finish what she started," D added grimly.

That was a disturbing thought.

"We need more evidence," Mark said, pushing his plate to the side. "Right now we're just speculating based on emotions you sensed during a completely different situation."

He was right, and I knew it. But I couldn't shake the feeling that the conflict over the Reeves family was connected to Amalia's murder somehow. The timing felt too coincidental—a retreat specifically called to address Amalia's concerns about other council members' methods, right after she'd objected to their approach with Marcus.

"What about the mysterious cabin guest?" D asked. "Should we be investigating him?"

"Probably," I said. "Though if he's been staying here for over a week, he's probably not connected to the council retreat. We don't even know if he's a witch or shifter. A plain human couldn't have done this."

"Unless they're connected to one of the council members personally," Mark pointed out. "I mean, obviously not a plain human, but someone not on the council."

Another possibility I hadn't considered. What if someone had arranged for backup support, or what if one of the council members had personal reasons for wanting privacy during the retreat?

"This is getting complicated again," I said, pushing my half-eaten breakfast away.

"You've done enough of them to know murder investigations usually are," Mark said sympathetically. "But you're doing better than you think. We have suspects, we have timelines, and we have a general idea of motive. That's more than a lot of investigations start with."

I hoped he was right, because I was starting to feel like I was drowning in possibilities rather than narrowing down to solutions.

"What's our next step?" D asked.

"I think we need to talk to the mysterious cabin guest," I said. "And we need to find out more about what happened during that evening discussion. If there really were loud, angry voices, someone's lying about how professional and calm things were."

"And Maria?" Mark asked.

"Maria too. But carefully. If she did kill Amalia, accidentally or otherwise, I don't want to spook her into doing something desperate. We don't have any proof pointing to her either, so let's keep open minds."

22

After breakfast, we decided to conduct more thorough interviews with the remaining council members. The first round had been focused on establishing basic timelines and alibis, but now I wanted to dig deeper into the relationships and conflicts within the group.

"We should start with Robert Kim," Mark suggested as we set up in the small meeting room again. "He seemed nervous during the first interview, but not evasive."

"And he was staying right next door to Amalia," I added. "If anyone heard something that night, it would be him."

We called Robert in first. He looked even more nervous than he had the day before, fidgeting with his cufflinks and glancing around the room like he expected someone to jump out at him.

"Mr. Kim," I said, trying to sound reassuring, "we just have a few follow-up questions. Nothing too formal."

"Of course," he said, though his emotional state suggested he was anything but relaxed about it.

"Yesterday you mentioned that the evening discussion

was about developing better protocols," Mark said. "Can you be more specific about what was discussed?"

Robert shifted in his chair. "Well, there were different opinions about how to handle situations like the one with the Reeves family. I suppose that's the most recent and clear example."

"What kind of different opinions?"

"Some felt we should maintain stronger boundaries with families who might cause exposure risks. Others thought we should be more... collaborative. Amalia wasn't the only voice raised."

We needed a better understanding of the allegiances. "Which side were you on?" I asked.

"I tend to think community safety should be the priority," Robert said carefully. "But I understood Amalia's concerns about our methods. It is not a simple issue, Protector."

He wasn't wrong, but he didn't seem to see the distinction between what needed to be done—protect the community—and how you did it. "What concerns specifically?"

Robert hesitated, and I could sense him weighing how much to reveal. "Amalia felt that some council members were too quick to separate families instead of looking for alternatives. She thought we should work more closely with the protectors or possibly confer with other councils to find less drastic responses instead of trying to handle everything internally."

Given the way this council reacted, I didn't hold out hope for other ones finding a solution. "Did that cause tension during your discussion? More than differing opinions?"

"Some," Robert admitted. "Amalia could be quite passionate about her position."

"Passionate how?" Mark asked.

Robert looked uncomfortable. "I don't like to talk out of school, but you are the protector. She raised her voice. Said we were more interested in control than actual protection. It got a bit heated."

So the animals had been right about loud, angry voices. The evening discussion hadn't been nearly as professional as everyone had initially claimed. "Who did she specifically disagree with?" I asked.

Robert's emotional state spiked—definitely guilt and reluctance. "I don't want to speak ill of colleagues," he said.

I got it, I did, but nothing got solved without the truth. "Mr. Kim, someone murdered Amalia two nights ago. Speaking honestly about her relationships with other council members isn't speaking ill—it's helping us find her killer."

He winced at the word "killer" but nodded slowly. "Maria Santos disagreed with almost everything Amalia said. They've had philosophical differences for years, but that night... Maria accused Amalia of being naive about the dangers facing our community. Said her collaborative approach would get us all exposed and destroyed."

Finally, the truth. The relief in his emotions leaped out of his shields. "How did Amalia respond?"

"She said Maria was paranoid and controlling. That fear was making us forget we're supposed to be helping people, not imprisoning them." Robert shifted uncomfortably. "It wasn't their first argument about community management."

"What about the others? Did anyone else get involved in the argument?"

"James tried to mediate. Ormand just sat there looking disapproving. Helena looked like she wanted to disappear. Elizabeth kept trying to steer the conversation back to practical matters." Frustration seeped into the relief, a sickly yellow-green.

"What time did this argument happen?" I asked, not willing to let go now that he was talking.

"Around ten, maybe ten-fifteen. It went on for about twenty minutes before Elizabeth finally called an end to the evening session."

That timeline put the argument well after the supposed nine-thirty end to discussions, and it explained why someone might have been pacing outside afterward. "After the argument ended, what did everyone do?"

"Most people went straight to their rooms. I think Maria and Helena stayed behind for a few minutes—maybe to clean up or discuss something privately. I was too tired to pay much attention."

Mark took over, somehow sensing my need to digest the information rather than come up with the next question. "Did you hear anything unusual later that night?"

"Footsteps in the hallway around eleven-thirty, maybe midnight. Someone walking back and forth. I assumed it was just someone having trouble sleeping after all the tension."

"Thank you, Mr. Kim," I said. "You've been very helpful."

After Robert left, I looked at Mark and D.

"So much for professional discourse," D said before I could ask what they thought.

"Maria and Amalia had a serious public argument about the same issues they disagreed about during the Reeves situation," I said. "And Robert mentioned it's been going on for years."

"And Maria stayed behind after the argument ended," Mark added. "She had opportunity to approach Amalia later."

"But would she really kill someone over a philosophical disagreement?" I asked.

"People have killed for less," Mark said. "I've been reading some of the Vancouver Police Department case files to understand mainland crime patterns better."

I stared at him. "Those are public records?"

Mark looked slightly embarrassed. "Well, not exactly public..."

"I've been doing a little creative research," D admitted. "I may have found ways around some of their digital security. For educational purposes."

"You hacked the police database?"

"I prefer 'conducted unauthorized research,'" D said. "But yes. And Mark's right—people kill for surprisingly small reasons when they're already under stress."

I wasn't sure whether to be impressed or horrified by D's hacking skills, but I supposed it was useful information and I trusted him not to get caught. "Let's talk to James O'Brien next," I said. "See if his story matches Robert's. I mean, it's probably better to get more perspectives, right?"

James O'Brien entered the room with the same nervous energy he'd shown in the first interview, but he seemed more willing to talk than Robert had been at the beginning.

"I hope you're making progress," he said as he sat down. "This whole situation is terrible for everyone."

"We're learning more about what happened that evening," Mark said. "Can you tell us about the discussion you had after dinner?"

"It started professionally enough," James said. "But things got heated when we started talking about the Reeves situation and how we'd handled it."

"Heated how?" Mark asked.

"Amalia was upset about some of our methods. She felt

we'd been too controlling, too focused on separating the family instead of finding alternatives." James ran a hand through his hair. "She wasn't wrong, honestly. We could have handled it better."

"Who did she specifically criticize?" Mark asked, making a note. I watched for emotions while he collected answers.

"Mostly Maria, but also Elizabeth to some extent. Maria got defensive and accused Amalia of putting idealism ahead of community safety. It escalated from there."

Mark paused to make another note before asking, "What did you do when things got heated?"

"Tried to mediate, but honestly, they weren't listening to me. The argument had been building for months—this retreat was supposed to address it and stop the constant sniping, but instead it just brought everything to a head."

His take wasn't too far off on the details, but the interpretation was more subtle, like he didn't want us to know his true feelings.

"What time did the argument end?" Mark continued the interview.

"Around ten-thirty, I think. Elizabeth finally shut it down and sent everyone to their rooms."

That jibed with everything we knew so far.

"What did you do after that?" Mark asked.

"Went straight to my room. I was exhausted by all the conflict." James paused. "Though I did hear people talking in the hallway later—maybe around eleven? Couldn't make out words, but it sounded like two people having a quiet conversation."

That was new information. Robert hadn't mentioned voices, just footsteps.

Time for me to join in. "Could you tell who was talking?"

"No, but one voice sounded like it might have been

Maria. The other... I'm not sure. Could have been Amalia, but I can't be certain."

His emotions were firmly in control. I suspected it was because he didn't care. Not about the murder, but about the infighting. "How long did the conversation last?"

He waved a hand in dismissal. "Not long. Maybe five minutes? Then I heard a door close and everything went quiet."

After James left, we sat in silence for a moment.

"So according to James, Maria and possibly Amalia were having a quiet conversation in the hallway around eleven," I said. "That could be when Maria suggested they have tea to work things out."

"Or when she convinced Amalia to let her into the room," Mark added.

"The timeline is starting to make sense," D said. "Public argument at ten, private conversation at eleven, murder sometime after that."

"But James seemed genuinely uncertain about whether the second voice was Amalia," I pointed out. "What if Maria was talking to someone else?"

"Like who?" D asked.

"I don't know. But we should keep our options open." These interviews were taking too long. I wanted to go look at this mysterious cabin and talk to whoever was inside.

They weren't a complete waste of time. I was starting to feel like we were building a solid case against Maria, but something about it still felt incomplete. We had no real proof against anyone, and I might not be able to identify it, but there was a giant hole in our knowledge somewhere.

23

Ormand Mistry entered the meeting room radiating controlled composure like a CEO meeting with his board. Outwardly calm and confident, inside he was a whirl of contradictions. His shield couldn't contain the roiling mess. He sat down across from us and folded his hands precisely.

"Mr. Mistry," I said, "we've been talking to the other council members about the evening discussion two nights ago. We'd like to hear your perspective and your personal position on the topic."

"Certainly, though I should mention that I prefer to observe rather than participate in... emotional discussions." His words were delivered in a gentle voice. His emotions spiked with worry and regret.

"You stayed out of the argument between Maria and Amalia?" I asked.

"I don't consider shouting matches to be productive. When colleagues choose to air personal grievances in public, I find it's best to remain neutral."

"Personal grievances?" Mark asked. "I thought this was about community policy."

Ormand's expression didn't change, but I caught a flicker of something like disdain in his aura. "Policy disagreements become personal when people let emotions override professional judgment. Maria and Amalia had been building toward that confrontation for months."

"What did you think of their respective positions?" I asked.

"Both had valid points. Amalia's collaborative approach has merit in theory. Maria's concerns about security are practical and well-founded." He paused. "However, I found Maria's delivery... unnecessarily aggressive. Perhaps if she had been more open to kindness, we would not be here now."

"Aggressive how?" I asked.

"She accused Amalia of being dangerously naive. Suggested that Amalia's methods would destroy everything our community has built. It was quite personal, really." He looked down at his hands folded in his lap. "Drama does not lead to solutions."

He was right there. "And Amalia's response?"

"Equally personal. She called Maria paranoid and accused her of using fear to justify authoritarian methods." Ormand smoothed his already-perfect tie. His emotions calmed as we asked questions. "Both allowed their emotions to compromise their professional judgment. As I said, personal issues."

There went my naive expectation that wisdom came with age. The way Ormand put it, the two women acted like teenagers fighting over a boyfriend. "Did you hear anything unusual later that night?"

"Some movement in the hallway, but I retired early and had little interest in monitoring my colleagues' activities."

I studied Ormand's emotions as he spoke. Now that he'd settled his anxious thoughts, I could tell he was definitely holding back, but it felt more like professional discretion than guilt. He genuinely seemed to disapprove of both Maria and Amalia's behavior. That didn't help me slot him into an ally or foe position, and I needed to do that so I could assess the value of his information.

"Mr. Mistry, do you think Maria was genuinely angry enough to... do something drastic about her disagreement with Amalia?"

Ormand considered this with the same careful precision he seemed to apply to everything. "Maria Santos is a passionate advocate for her beliefs. Sometimes that passion overrides her better judgment." He met my eyes directly. "Do I think she's capable of violence when she believes the community is threatened? Yes, I do."

"That's a serious accusation," Mark said.

"You asked for my professional assessment, and I've provided it. Maria has always believed that extreme situations require extreme measures. This retreat was supposed to be about reining in her more... dramatic tendencies. Don't let the others tell you it was about collaboration. Maria had pushed too hard."

After Ormand left, we sat in silence for a moment. Unlike Robert's nervous revelations or James's conflicted observations, Ormand had delivered his assessment with little emotion.

"Well," D said finally, "that was damning."

"He basically said Maria is capable of murder if she thinks it's justified," I said.

"And that this retreat was specifically about controlling

her 'dramatic tendencies,'" Mark added. "That suggests a pattern of escalating behavior."

I thought about everything we'd learned. Maria's heated argument with Amalia. Her staying behind after the session ended. The possible hallway conversation. Her history of philosophical conflicts with Amalia dating back to the Reeves situation.

"It has to be Maria," I said. "Everything points to her."

"The evidence is certainly compelling," Mark agreed. "Motive, opportunity, and a pattern of escalating conflict."

"But?" D asked, picking up on my hesitation.

"But it feels... too neat somehow. Like we're being led to the obvious conclusion."

"Sometimes the obvious conclusion is the right one," Mark said. "Not every murder is a complicated conspiracy—at least that's what I've seen on TV."

We weren't getting anywhere, and I had another source. "Destroyer, have you learned anything that will help?"

"I have learned many things. Whether they will help or not, even I, the emperor of many lands, cannot tell."

I wasn't sure if he wanted praise or was just playing for dramatic effect. "Tell me—perhaps I will know."

"The isolated dwelling in the forest contains a witch."

I nearly dropped my coffee cup. "What?" Mark and D looked at me like I'd gone crazy. "Destroyer says the person in the cabin is a witch."

"What else does he know?" Mark asked.

I asked them to wait, saying I couldn't be sure. "How can you tell?" I thought at Destroyer.

"I am not ready to reveal all of my capabilities. In this case, I see power. Do not ask for more."

I looked at Mark and D, who were watching me with curiosity. "Definitely a witch. Apparently my familiar can see power, but I have been ordered to keep my curiosity about that to myself." We'd be having a long talk when this was over.

"A witch who's been here for over a week," Mark said slowly. "Someone who's been watching the council's activities and hiding their magical abilities."

"Someone who might have a completely different motive for killing Amalia," D added.

My carefully constructed case against Maria suddenly felt a lot less certain. We'd been so focused on the council members and their internal conflicts that we'd ignored the possibility of an outside threat.

"I guess we've been looking at things that prove our theory, and it's too early for that. We need to talk to this cabin guest," I said. "Right now."

"Wait," Mark said. "If this person is a hidden witch who's been observing the council, approaching them directly could be dangerous. We don't know what their intentions are."

"But we can't just leave them alone either. If they killed Amalia, they might be planning to kill other council members."

"Or they might be completely innocent and just value their privacy," D pointed out.

"Only one way to find out," I said, standing up.

24

Befote we headed to the cabin to confront the mysterious witch, I wanted to gather as much information as possible about what we might be walking into. The last thing we needed was to surprise someone who might be dangerous. No matter what kind of defensive spell any of us could cast—and I had none to hand—I wasn't going in guns blazing, metaphorically.

"I should check with Destroyer and the local animals," I said to Mark and D. "See what they've observed about this cabin guest."

"Good idea," Mark said. "The more we know, the better."

I stepped outside and found a quiet spot near the edge of the forest where I could talk to animals without being overheard by hotel guests. I didn't know if their fear would keep them in the deeper trees, but despite what I'd been told, plenty of birds and small creatures seemed to hang out near the lodge.

"Destroyer," I thought at him, "tell me what you've learned about the witch in the cabin."

"The local birds are disappointingly unhelpful," he

replied with obvious frustration. "I have attempted to organize them into a proper reconnaissance network, but they lack discipline and strategic thinking. It is as though they don't value being part of my empire."

Did I have to explain free will to him? I suppressed the thought before he could grab onto it. "What exactly did they tell you?"

"That they avoid the cabin area because the human throws things at them when they get too close. Beyond that, they claim to have seen nothing useful. Stubborn and cowardly creatures."

He had no experience of being hunted. I'd talk to him later about compassion, but right now I needed his information. "Despite the resistance to your rule, did anyone describe the witch?"

"Male, not old, not young. Hair like an abandoned nest. Dark stains on his hands and clothes. Some of the items thrown were notebooks, though the squirrels were not bright enough to know that word. The witch retrieved these immediately."

A writer or artist, maybe? That might explain why he wanted privacy and didn't want housekeeping services. He probably didn't intend to use the books as weapons. "It would be nice to have an idea why he's hiding."

"The local animals will never gain that skill. One of your council members visited him. Last dark, the raccoon said."

That was helpful—or at least something we could follow up on. "Which council member?"

"The one with silver hair arranged in an aggressive manner."

Maria? So had the witch been nervous about Maria specifically?

I caught a twitch of a tail and spotted Nutkin watching

me from a nearby tree. He scampered down when I waved. "Have you learned anything new about the witch in the cabin?" I asked him. I told Destroyer to stay away so the squirrel wouldn't feel intimidated.

"Yes! I recruited a mouse to help with surveillance." Nutkin's tail twitched with excitement. "She can get much closer to the dwelling than the rest of us."

I crossed my fingers. "What did she find out?"

"The human talks to himself constantly, like there's another person in the room. But my mouse investigator confirms he's always alone."

Maybe it was more like a mental illness. Did witches develop things like schizophrenia? "Does he seem dangerous?"

"Nervous, mostly. Like when a moose stomps around my territory—I jump and hide until it's safe to come out."

"Watching for anything specific?" I wondered aloud. I didn't think Nutkin or his mouse could make sense of this behavior.

"My mouse says he was jumpier when the silver-haired witch was walking around outside. He was watching her through the big eyes thing and he talked to himself until she left."

I'd ask this mystery witch what that was about. Since I'd been surprised by the depth of Nutkin's answer, I asked, "Anything else?"

"Someone came to the cabin," Nutkin said. "A witch."

Maria? "Could you see who it was?"

"We don't know names. Tall, skinny like a baby deer. Long hair. Cabin witch didn't like the new one."

Two visitors? The raccoon couldn't have been so wrong in his description. And I hadn't seen a tall, skinny witch.

"Thank you," I said to Nutkin. "You and your mouse have been incredibly helpful."

I walked back to where Mark and D were waiting.

"What did you learn?" D asked.

I updated them on everything—well, not Destroyer's side comments, but all the details.

"Another visitor? Someone we don't know about?" Mark said. "That could be significant."

"Yes, another witch in the area means another suspect. There's something else," I said. "We'll need to check the timing when we interview him. I'm not sure if Maria came first, but I think I might know who the other witch is."

"So he's specifically afraid of Maria, or specifically interested in her," D said. "That's something—I just don't know what."

"Either way, it suggests a connection between them," Mark added. "And maybe Maria sent the second visitor."

I thought about the timeline. The cabin guest had been here for over a week, watching the hotel. Maria and the council had arrived for their retreat. Amalia was murdered. And now we discovered that the cabin guest had been specifically monitoring Maria's activities.

"There's another possibility," I said slowly. "What if the cabin guest isn't connected to Amalia's murder at all? What if he's here because of something else entirely?"

"Such as?" Mark asked.

"What if he's hiding from something or someone? And what if that someone showed up yesterday evening? Our tall, skinny witch."

Mark looked interested. "You mean she might have been the person he was hiding from?"

"It's possible. Nutkin said the cabin guest seemed surprised and unhappy to see his visitor."

"But how does that connect to Amalia's murder?" D asked.

"Maybe it doesn't," I said. "Maybe we have two separate situations happening at the same time—Maria killing Amalia over their policy disagreements, and a hidden witch dealing with his own problems."

"Or maybe the situations are connected in ways we don't understand yet," Mark said. "Or maybe Maria isn't the killer? These two new witches could be framing her."

I tried to think through the possibilities. A hidden witch watching the hotel for over a week. Specifically monitoring Maria. An unwelcome visitor yesterday evening. Amalia murdered two nights ago.

"We need to talk to him," I said. "Even if he's not connected to Amalia's murder, he might have seen something useful. And if he is connected..."

"Then we need to know what his agenda is," Mark finished. "Even if he's not a killer, we need to be sure."

As we headed toward the forest path that would take us to the cabin, I couldn't shake the feeling that we were about to discover something that would change our understanding of this entire situation.

"Destroyer," I called silently, "keep an eye on the hotel while we're gone. Let me know if anyone leaves or if anything unusual happens."

25

W e were halfway to the forest path when Toni from the front desk came hurrying after us, looking flustered.

"Ms. Fortuna! Ms. Santos is asking for you urgently. She said it's about... arrangements that can't wait."

I looked at Mark and D with frustration. We'd been so close to getting answers, and now we were being summoned back to deal with more council drama.

"Did she say what kind of arrangements?" Mark asked.

"No," Toni said. "I didn't want to pry. Ms. Santos just said it was urgent that someone find you. I saw you headed this way, so I took a chance."

"We should go," D said reluctantly. "If they're getting impatient enough to send hotel staff after us, it must be important."

I sighed, casting one last look toward the forest path. The cabin would have to wait.

When we returned to the conference room, the entire council was there, looking more tense than I'd seen them since we'd arrived. Elizabeth was standing at the head of the table like she was chairing a board meeting, and everyone else wore grim expressions.

"Ms. Fortuna," Elizabeth said without preamble, "we need to discuss Amalia's funeral arrangements. The situation has become urgent."

"Funeral arrangements?" I asked. "I thought we were focused on finding her killer."

"We are," Helena said. "But the concealment spells won't hold indefinitely. It's been two days since you arrived, and the cover story isn't holding up."

Couldn't they keep up the pretense? "What does that mean?"

"The hotel employees are already suggesting that we have a doctor come and treat Amalia. They feel... well, they say they're concerned about her, but I believe it's more about liability."

"We need to resolve the situation with Amalia's body," Elizabeth said. "We've contacted her friends and colleagues, and they're expecting a memorial service tomorrow evening."

"Here?" I asked. "At the lodge?"

"In the forest clearing behind the property," Maria said. "We've already made arrangements with the hotel management for a private evening event. They think it's a corporate team-building exercise. We will tell them that Amalia went home when we are done."

I stared at them. "You want to bury Amalia tomorrow night while we're still investigating her murder?"

"We don't have a choice," James O'Brien said. "The concealment spells we used rely on people believing the story. Now that they are questioning things, the illusion is breaking down. I hate to think what will happen if her death is exposed."

"Besides," Ormand added with his usual precision, "Amalia had no living relatives. Her friends have already arranged to travel here for the service. Canceling now would raise questions we can't answer."

Questions they didn't want to bother answering. I wanted to snap back with a lecture about responsibility, but reprimanding them wouldn't help, at least not right now.

"How many people are we talking about?" Mark asked, clearly impatient to get on with our plan.

"About thirty," Helena said. "Magical community members from Vancouver and Seattle. They'll arrive tomorrow afternoon."

Thirty more witches arriving at the hotel. Thirty more potential suspects, witnesses, or complications. This investigation was getting more complex by the hour. "Are these newcomers planning to stay?"

Maria made a noise of frustration, but I couldn't tell what triggered it. Everyone's shields had been reinforced. "Of course not. They will leave after the ceremony. They have chartered a bus."

I wasn't sure if that was good or bad, but it was already arranged. "What exactly are you asking me to do?"

"Give us permission to proceed with the burial," Elizabeth said. "You've bound us here with the council oath, so we need your authorization to make these arrangements."

I looked around the table at their expectant faces. Even without my power, I could read expressions. They all seemed genuinely concerned about the concealment spells failing, but there was something else underneath their urgency. Relief, maybe? Were they hoping that burying Amalia would somehow end the investigation?

"I don't know," I said honestly. "Burying the victim seems like it might interfere with the investigation."

"You have already examined the body and her room," Maria pointed out. "I assume you have magical residue samples, timeline information, and witness statements. What more could be learned from... keeping her around?"

When she put it like that, it sounded reasonable. But something about the timing felt wrong. "Why tomorrow night specifically?"

"Because that's when Amalia's friends will be here," Helena said. "They're expecting a proper memorial service. We can't exactly tell them we're postponing because we're investigating her murder."

Interesting way of putting it. "What do they think happened to her?"

"Natural causes," Robert said. "A heart problem that developed suddenly during the retreat."

So the cover story was already in place, and people were traveling based on that information. Changing plans now would definitely raise questions. Did I want that?

"Ms. Fortuna," Elizabeth said, "I understand your reluctance, but we're dealing with community security on a much larger scale than just this investigation. If the concealment spells fail and mundane authorities get involved, it could expose magical communities across the entire Pacific Northwest."

That was a compelling argument. My job as protector was supposed to be about protecting the magical world, not just solving individual crimes.

"How long do the concealment spells have?" I asked.

"Maybe another day," Helena said. "Two at the absolute most, as long as the hotel management doesn't get proactive."

"And if we bury Amalia tomorrow night?"

"Then we can remove the spell after casting a cleansing," Elizabeth explained.

"You're sure there's nothing more to be learned from examining the body?" I really needed to find a spell that broke through people's shields. I hated the thought of violating anyone's privacy, but in a murder investigation, speed was more important than individual privacy.

"Quite sure," Maria said firmly.

I looked at Mark, hoping he'd have some insight about whether this was normal investigative procedure.

"It's not ideal," he said carefully, "but if the alternative is magical exposure on a large scale, it might be necessary."

"What if we haven't solved the case by tomorrow night?" I asked. I hoped we'd be done well before the new witches arrived.

"Then we solve it afterward," Ormand said pragmatically. "The killer will still be the killer whether Amalia is buried or not."

That was technically true, but it felt like giving up on an important part of the investigation. "I need to think about this," I said.

"There isn't much time to think," Elizabeth said. "Amalia's friends are already preparing to travel. Some are already on the way to rendezvous points."

"How convenient," Destroyer observed in my mind. "They have created a situation where you must choose between solving the murder and preventing magical exposure."

"You think they're manipulating me?" What a stupid question. Of course at least one of them was.

"In my empire, no one would be allowed to interfere with the protector."

I didn't want to be a dictator. "All right," I said finally.

"The funeral can proceed tomorrow night. But the investigation continues afterward, and no one leaves until we've identified the killer."

"Of course," Elizabeth said, though I caught a flicker of something that might have been relief.

"And I want to be involved in all the funeral arrangements," I added. "If thirty new witches are coming to the hotel, I need to know who they are and why they're here."

"Naturally," Helena said.

As the council members dispersed to make their arrangements, I couldn't shake the feeling that I'd just been maneuvered into something I didn't fully understand.

"You look troubled," Mark said.

"I don't like being rushed," I said. "And I don't like the way they presented this as an emergency that requires immediate action."

"But if the concealment spells really are failing..." D said.

"Then we deal with it. But I'm not convinced they're telling us the whole truth about the timeline."

"What do you want to do?"

I looked toward the window that faced the forest. Somewhere out there, a mysterious witch was hiding in a cabin, possibly with answers that could solve this entire case. Or simply a waste of time that had nothing to do with Amalia.

"We need to talk to the cabin guest," I said. "Before thirty more witches arrive and complicate everything even further."

"Now?" Mark asked.

"Right now. Before the council thinks of another emergency that requires our immediate attention or finds a way to distract us."

26

A fter the council meeting, I felt like I needed to double-check something before we proceeded with letting them bury Amalia tomorrow night.

"Before we go, I want to examine the body one more time," I said to Mark and D as we headed back toward the rooms. "Make sure we haven't missed anything that might be important."

"Good idea," Mark said. "Once she's buried, we lose access to any physical evidence."

"And if we're letting thirty more witches into the hotel tomorrow, we should be absolutely certain about what we know," D added. "We don't want anyone thinking the protector doesn't know what she's doing."

We made our way back to Amalia's room. The wards were still in place, but they felt different somehow—weaker, maybe, or more unstable. Helena hadn't been lying about the concealment spells requiring more energy to maintain.

Mark opened the door and we stepped inside. The room looked exactly as we'd left it, with Amalia still sitting in the chair by the window. But something felt different.

"Do you smell that?" I asked.

Mark sniffed the air. "Faint perfume. Floral, but not the kind of thing you'd expect in a hotel room."

"Someone's been in here," D said, moving carefully around the room. "Recently."

I reached out with my emotion-reading ability, trying to sense any residual feelings in the space. There was definitely something new—anxiety mixed with guilt, and the lingering trace of someone who'd been moving quickly and quietly.

"Whoever it was, they were nervous about being here," I said.

Mark was examining the area around Amalia's chair more carefully. "Look at this."

On the floor beside the chair, partially hidden under the edge of the bed skirt, was a small silver earring. It definitely hadn't been there during our first examination of the scene.

"Someone dropped this," Mark said, carefully picking it up with a tissue.

I studied the earring. It was simple but elegant, the kind of thing a professional woman might wear to important meetings. "Do you recognize it?"

"I think so," D said slowly. "I'm pretty sure I saw Maria wearing earrings like this yesterday."

We all looked at each other. If Maria had been in this room recently, that was highly suspicious behavior for someone who was supposedly innocent.

"Why would she come back here?" I asked.

"Maybe she was looking for something," Mark suggested. "Or maybe she was trying to plant evidence to frame someone else."

"Or remove evidence that might implicate her," I added.

"Although the evidence points to someone trying to implicate her."

"We need to confront her about this," D said. "If she's innocent, we'll know by her reaction."

"Agreed, but carefully," Mark said. "If she's the killer and she knows we're onto her, she might do something desperate."

As we prepared to leave the room, something occurred to me. "Wait," I said. "What about Beatrix Dai?" I'd completely forgotten my suspicion that she was the second visitor.

"The intelligence officer who's investigating the tea source?" Mark asked.

"Exactly. She's been gone this whole time, but she must have some kind of timeline for her investigation. Shouldn't we be getting reports from her? And didn't someone text her to come back?"

D pulled out his phone and checked his notes. "Actually, that's a good point. You did ask for her to be recalled."

"It's odd that she hasn't updated anyone, but we're assuming that. What if someone is holding back?" Mark said. "And it's only been a day—maybe she was too far away to get here sooner."

True. The actual time passing wasn't much. This was only the second day, and I should keep that in mind. "What if she's not actually investigating the tea source?" I said slowly. "What if she's the mysterious visitor that the cabin guest had yesterday evening? It means she's back, but no one has told us."

"You think Beatrix is connected to the hidden witch somehow?" D asked. "Like she's working two cases?"

"It's possible. If she's the council's intelligence officer, she might know things about magical security that the rest of us don't," Mark said. "And maybe she's not just working for the Vancouver council. We really need to talk to her."

"But why would she visit the cabin secretly?" D asked.

"Maybe she's investigating him as a potential threat to the council. Or maybe she knows who he is and why he's hiding," I said. Too much guessing. We needed answers to keep us on the right track.

Mark looked thoughtful. "If Beatrix is involved in this somehow, we need to talk to her before the funeral tomorrow. She might have information that changes everything."

"How do we find her?" I asked.

"Ask the council?" D said. "Yes, they might lie, but Mark's power will tell us if they do."

"I guess we pretend we don't suspect she's here," I said. "And I can demand every council member be present for the ceremony."

As Mark sealed the room with official crime scene wards that would preserve any remaining evidence and keep the distraction spell running, I thought about what we'd discovered. Maria's earring in Amalia's room was damning evidence, but the missing intelligence officer was equally suspicious. "This case keeps getting more complicated," I said.

"Maybe," Mark said, "or maybe we're finally starting to see all the pieces. Maria as the killer, Beatrix as someone who knows more than she's saying, and the cabin guest as a witness who's been hiding from whatever Beatrix represents. Or each one of them could fit in any of those roles."

"You think they're all connected?" I wanted some concrete clues to hold onto. This constant "it could be this person or that" was just dragging things out.

"I think we have too many coincidences for them not to

be connected somehow," Mark said, leading the way toward the lobby.

I tried to organize everything in my mind. Maria had apparently been in Amalia's room recently and left incriminating evidence—by accident? Beatrix had disappeared but maybe not. And tomorrow night, thirty more witches would arrive for a funeral that might be designed to bury more than just Amalia's body.

"We need to move faster," I said. "Too many things are happening at once for us to investigate them all properly."

"Which should we prioritize?" D asked.

"All of them," I said. "We talk to the cabin guest this afternoon, we demand that Beatrix return immediately, and we confront Maria about the earring tonight."

"That's a lot for one day," Mark said.

"Then we'd better get started."

27

I decided to approach the cabin alone first. If he really was a hidden witch who'd been watching the hotel for over a week, showing up with Mark and D might seem threatening. Better to make initial contact by myself and assess the situation before bringing in backup.

"Are you sure about going alone?" Mark asked as we reached the edge of the forest.

"I'll be fine," I said, trying to project more confidence than I felt. "If he's been hiding here this long, he's probably more scared than dangerous."

"Call us if you need anything," D said. "We'll be close enough to hear you if you shout."

The path to the cabin wound through dense forest, and I could see why someone might choose this location for privacy. The trees were thick enough that if you didn't know it was here, you'd never come looking. As I got closer, I could feel emotions bursting from the building. Agitation, fear, remorse, and about six other shades I didn't have time to sort out.

The cabin itself was rustic but well-maintained. The

clearing opened out and a gravel path led to the porch. I climbed the three steps to the front door and knocked.

"Go away," a man shouted. "I don't need housekeeping or maintenance or anything else."

"I'm not hotel staff," I called. "My name is Cossi Fortuna. I'm a protector investigating some incidents at the hotel."

There was a long pause, then footsteps approached slowly. The door opened to reveal a man who looked exactly as Destroyer had described—wild hair that did resemble an abandoned bird's nest, ink stains on his fingers and clothes, and an intense, nervous energy that could only come from too much caffeine and not enough sleep.

"A protector?" he said, looking me up and down. "You're very young for a protector."

"Yes," I admitted without adding anything that could sound defensive. I had to stop reacting like that statement was a put-down. "Could I come in? I have some questions about what you might have observed at the hotel."

He stepped back reluctantly. "I suppose you'd better. Though I should warn you, I'm not exactly... I mean, I know why you're here."

The interior of the cabin was chaos. Papers covered every available surface, notebooks were stacked in precarious towers, and the walls were covered with what looked like hand-drawn maps and charts. It looked like the workspace of someone obsessed with a complex project.

His emotions were settling now. I think his last words brought him some relief, like it was over, whatever it was. I didn't want to jump to conclusions because I'd done that with Maria, and it was proving difficult to keep my options open.

"You're a researcher?" I asked, taking in the scene.

"Was," he said, wringing his hands nervously. "Before

everything went wrong. Look, I know why you're here, and I want you to know that I'm prepared to confess."

I stared at him. He wasn't even willing to wait for me to ask, but I did. "Confess to what?"

"To my crime. But first, I need assurances that I won't be stripped of my magic."

"Stripped of your magic?" I couldn't hide my shock. "That's pretty drastic. Why do you think we'd punish you that harshly?" Prison was enough for the killers I'd already found. I knew magic stripping was possible, but very rarely used.

"Of course it is. It's the standard punishment for magical crimes that expose the community." He looked at me with confusion. "You're a protector and you don't know that?"

I was starting to feel seriously out of my depth. But if he was ready to confess to what he'd done, that meant all our investigation into Maria and the council conflicts had been wrong. Maria wasn't the killer after all. There was no way I'd let them strip his power.

"Before we proceed," I said carefully, "I need to call my associates to witness your confession. This is too important for me to handle alone."

"Call whoever you need to call," he said, slumping into a chair covered with papers. "I'm tired of hiding."

I stepped outside and texted Mark and D. "Get to the cabin immediately. The guest wants to confess."

"We'll be right there," Mark replied.

When I went back inside, the man was staring out the window with a haunted expression.

"Can you tell me your name?" I asked, settling into the only chair not covered in papers.

"Lionel Zimmer," he said. "I've been a researcher for the Kelowna magical community for fifteen years. Specialized in historical magical practices and their applications to modern community security."

"That sounds like important work." Why would he want to kill Amalia?

"It was, until I made a mistake that could have..." He trailed off, looking at me uncertainly. "You already know about that, don't you? The councils talk to each other about these things."

Less than he thought, but that wasn't what I needed to talk about. "Why don't you tell me in your own words?"

"I was trying to help," he said, his voice full of self-recrimination. "I thought I'd found something that could protect our communities better. But I was wrong about the power levels, and suddenly there were plain humans involved who shouldn't have been."

My stomach clenched with fear and the memory of what Phillip accused my mother of doing—just that, exposing the witches and shifters to the plain humans. Did Amalia know he'd done it? "When did this happen?"

"Last month. The Kelowna council has been trying to figure out damage control ever since." Lionel ran his hands through his already-disheveled hair. "When I saw the Vancouver council arrive here, I knew they must have found out about it."

So he ran? "Is that why you've been hiding?"

"I couldn't face it. The punishment, the exile, living without magic." He looked up at me with desperate eyes. "But then I realized that hiding was just making everything worse. Someone had to take responsibility."

I was getting more confused, not less. "Lionel, what exactly are you confessing to?"

"You know what I did. Why else would a protector be here investigating?" He gestured helplessly at the chaos of papers around us. "I've been trying to figure out how to prove I can fix it without doing more damage, but I can't—more spells will just reinforce the memories."

Before I could respond, I heard footsteps approaching the cabin. Mark and D had arrived. "That will be my associates," I said. "Are you ready to give your statement?"

Lionel nodded grimly. "I've been ready since the moment I realized what a mess I'd made."

As Mark and D knocked on the door, I realized that I might have been completely wrong about everything. If Lionel was confessing to some kind of magical exposure incident, then maybe Amalia's murder was connected to that somehow. But I still didn't understand how it all fit together. And since neither Mrs. V nor I knew about this event, how bad could it be?

"Come in," I called. Mark and D entered the cabin.

"This is Lionel Zimmer," I said. "He has something he wants to tell us."

Lionel looked at the three of us and took a deep breath. "I suppose there's no point in putting it off any longer."

28

M ark immediately took charge of the questioning, pulling out his notebook. "Mr. Zimmer," he said, settling into a professional stance, "before you begin, please remember that we need the whole story. If we are to make the right decisions, we can't have holes in our information."

"Of course," Lionel said, though he looked confused by the formal tone. "I mean, that's why you're here, isn't it?"

"Why don't you start by telling us exactly what happened," Mark continued. "Take your time, and don't leave out any details."

Lionel glanced between the three of us, seeming to gather his courage. "Well, it started about a month ago. I was researching historical protection spells, trying to adapt them for modern use. I thought I'd found something promising in some old texts."

"Go on," Mark said when Lionel paused.

"I needed to test it, but I couldn't do that in Kelowna without raising questions. So I decided to try it some-where with good cover." Lionel's hands were shaking slightly. "The Renaissance Faire in Vancouver seemed perfect."

This wasn't going toward a murder confession.

"What exactly did you test?" D asked.

"Love potions," Lionel said miserably.

Mark's pen stopped moving. "Love potions? How is that a way to protect the community?"

"Well, not real love potions, of course. They don't actually exist. But I thought if I could create something that would make plain humans more agreeable and cooperative, it might be useful for community protection."

Changing people's attitudes with magic was never helpful. I mean, protectors could do it, but as far as I knew, none of us did it lightly. And the spell didn't always stick if the person's beliefs were entrenched. There were a few stories in the research material that scared me.

"I sold them as novelty items at the faire. You know how gullible plain humans can be about magical things. They bought dozens of them." Lionel buried his face in his hands. "I thought it was harmless. Just sugar water with a mild charm to make people feel good about themselves."

I stared at him. "That's what you're confessing to? Selling fake love potions?"

"Fake?" Lionel looked up, startled. "They weren't fake! That's the problem! I miscalculated the charm strength, and suddenly people were actually feeling the effects. Not real love, obviously, but enhanced attraction and cooperation. Some of them started posting about it online, saying they'd found 'real magic' at the faire."

"But nobody died?" D asked slowly. "And the effects wore off?"

"Died?" Lionel's eyes went wide with horror. "Of course nobody died! What kind of monster do you think I am?"

Well, he did expect his powers to be stripped.

Mark and I exchanged glances. "Mr. Zimmer," Mark said carefully, "we're investigating a murder that happened at the hotel two nights ago. We thought you were confessing to that."

"A murder?" Lionel shot to his feet, papers scattering. "You think I killed someone? I would never—I mean, my mistake was serious, but I'm not a killer!"

"Then why were you so worried about being stripped of your magic?" I asked.

"Because magical exposure is a serious crime! Even accidental exposure!" Lionel was pacing now, clearly agitated. "The Kelowna council has been trying to figure out how to handle the damage control. There are dozens of plain humans who think they experienced real magic."

"But you said councils talk to each other about these things," D pointed out. "How did you know we were here about your situation?"

"I didn't know for sure," Lionel admitted. "But when I saw the Vancouver council arrive, and then a protector showed up asking questions... I assumed word had gotten out."

Mark was making rapid notes. "Mr. Zimmer, we've had reports that you had visitors. Who was that?"

"Beatrix Dai. She's on the Vancouver council—intelligence gathering, I think. She was here investigating something else entirely, but she'd heard about my situation through council communications." Lionel looked embarrassed. "She convinced me I should turn myself in to the Kelowna council before she had to report me officially."

"What was she investigating?" I asked, hoping his answer would confirm the tea story.

"Something about contaminated tea, I think. She

mentioned it was related to the Vancouver council's retreat." Lionel shrugged. "She didn't give me details, but she said it was serious enough that my little problem was going to have to wait."

So Beatrix really had been investigating the tea source, just as the council claimed. That eliminated one of my suspicions about her involvement.

"Mr. Zimmer," Mark said, "I need to contact your council to arrange for your pickup. In the meantime, you'll need to remain in this cabin."

"Am I under arrest?"

"You're being confined pending transfer to your own council's jurisdiction," Mark said diplomatically. "It should only take a few hours. Do you have a contact number for someone there, or do I need to go through official channels?"

While Mark made the arrangements, I tried to process what we'd learned. Lionel wasn't the killer—his "crime" was selling love potions that worked a little too well. Beatrix really had been investigating the tea, not covering up murders. And we were back to suspecting Maria as our most likely killer, although I guess Beatrix could still be the killer.

"I'm sorry for the confusion," Lionel said to me as Mark talked on the phone. "I really thought you were here about the faire incident."

"It's not your fault," I said. "We're dealing with multiple situations happening at the same time."

"Is there anything I can do to help with your investigation? I mean, I have been watching the hotel for over a week."

That was a good point. Even if Lionel wasn't the killer, he might have seen something useful. "Actually, yes," I said.

"Can you tell us what you observed the night before last? Anything unusual around the hotel?"

"There was quite a bit of activity," Lionel said, settling back into his chair. "I saw two women having what looked like a heated argument on the back terrace around eleven. Then later, one of them was walking around outside, like she was trying to make a decision about something."

"Could you describe the women?"

"One had silver hair, very formally dressed. The other was younger, with shorter dark hair. The argument went on for maybe twenty minutes."

"Which one was walking around later?"

"The silver-haired woman. She paced for quite a while, then went back inside around midnight."

Mark finished his call and rejoined us. "The Kelowna council will send someone to collect Mr. Zimmer in about four hours. Until then, he's confined to the cabin."

"I understand," Lionel said. "And again, I'm sorry for the misunderstanding. I hope you find whoever really committed this murder. Living without my powers will be hard, but I deserve it."

Oops, I couldn't leave him with that impression. "No one is taking your magic," I said. "The exposure is confined to social media, right? It's probably long forgotten by now. And I'd bet money some of the people who were affected were on some kind of drug—lots of them will have the same effect. I will contact your council and discuss the appropriate punishment."

"What now?" D asked as we walked back toward the hotel.

"Now we confront Maria about the earring," I said. "And about her midnight walk."

"Before or after the funeral tomorrow night?" Mark asked.

No one could leave, so we didn't need to rush the interrogation. I was exhausted. Getting this solved fast was critical for all kinds of reasons, but mistakes happened when I ignored my needs. I thought about the thirty witches who would be arriving tomorrow, and the complexity that would add to an already complicated situation. I'd need to be fresh for that too.

"Tomorrow. We need to rest. First thing tomorrow."

29

The next morning was a rush of preparations for the memorial. We couldn't call it that or let any hint that the gathering was for Amalia because the hotel staff thought it was a celebration.

"We should approach Maria carefully about the earring," Mark said as we watched her talking to Helena and the lodge chef.

The decision to watch her before the confrontation should have helped. My power to read emotions wasn't getting much, but Maria was so busy she didn't remember to keep her shield in place all the time. "What do you mean?" I asked, though I had a feeling I knew where he was going.

"Helena has been our primary source of information about the council dynamics, and she's already lied to us multiple times," D pointed out. "And Beatrix's timeline still doesn't completely add up, even with Lionel's explanation."

I agreed, and if Maria had a good reason her jewelry was in the room, we'd be no further ahead. "You think we're being led toward Maria as a suspect?"

"It's possible," Mark said. "The earring could have been

planted. Or maybe Maria really did visit Amalia's room, but for reasons that had nothing to do with murder."

Before I could respond, I heard the rumble of a large vehicle pulling into the parking lot. Through the trees, I could see a charter bus with "Pacific Northwest Tours" printed on the side, maneuvering into a parking space.

"The memorial guests," I said with a sinking feeling. "They're arriving earlier than expected. We should have pulled Maria into a room for questioning before this."

D reached for his hot chocolate. "We still could."

Yes, but with so many people around, she could make it very difficult. "My instinct is to let the ceremony go ahead. I don't know why, except that Amalia deserves it. All our suspects are stuck here until I release them, so we can wait." And try to identify the killer with my power. Running around questioning everyone was important, but it didn't leave me time to act as the protector. I should have some kind of... feeling isn't the right word... about guilt. Maybe it only worked when the whole community was under threat.

Over the next hour, the hotel lobby transformed into a reunion scene as more than thirty witches greeted each other. It looked like many of the newcomers had friends in the Vancouver council. Not just Amalia's friends, but I saw Ormand uncharacteristically hug a tall red-haired witch like they'd been apart for a century.

We watched from our corner, trying to stay out of the way while observing the group dynamics. My mind kept being pulled back to how we'd handle this many witches and the case.

"Focus," Destroyer ordered me. "Even I, emperor of the world, cannot say who your killer is, but scattering your thoughts is unseemly for a protector."

Unseemly? Had he time-traveled to the Victorian era?

His words gave me comfort and a smile. "We'll know soon enough. Any interesting animal news?"

"I will be glad to return to my home domain. The witch in the cabin has left. The arrival of so many humans has caused my subjects to flee."

I knew Lionel was on his way back to Kelowna. I'd had an enlightening text discussion with one of his guards. Apparently, the council had cleaned up the "crisis." Lionel was often subject to melodramatic reactions. He would be on house arrest for a few weeks. No one was ever going to remove his magic.

Helena appeared at my elbow, looking harried but determined. I found myself studying her expression, wondering what she might be hiding. A little ray of frustration slipped through her shield.

"I want to thank you for agreeing to pause your investigation," she said. "I promise we will be available after the ceremony. We also want the killer found. Perhaps it doesn't always look that way, but we are busy people, and please remember most of the witches you've held here are innocent."

Nice to know she agreed that one of the council was the culprit.

"We're stuck," I said to Mark and D. "We can't do anything about the investigation until after the memorial ceremony. And I'm pretty sure we'll be told after it's over that everyone should rest."

"Maybe that's not entirely bad," Mark said thoughtfully. "We can observe all our suspects interacting with Amalia's friends. Sometimes killers reveal themselves when they're trying too hard to seem normal."

"And I won't let them push me off," I said. "If everyone is too tired, maybe they'll make a mistake."

"Excuse me," said a woman with silver-streaked hair pulled into a neat bun. "Are you Cossi Fortuna?"

"Yes, do I know you?" I knew the answer was no because she was completely unshielded. Her emotions were a mixture of sadness and admiration. Weird.

"No, I don't think so. I heard about you from a friend on Henbane. I wasn't able to come to the festival this year, or we would have met. You are the newest protector. I hear you have a very different view of our world. Margaret Simmons."

If stumbling around not knowing much was a different view, then yes. "Thank you. You were Amalia's friend?"

"For more years than I care to claim," Margaret said with a fond smile. "She was so inspiring. Always fighting for what she believed was right, even when it made her unpopular. She never could let something go if she thought it was unjust. I often wished I was more like her."

How could I be so stupid? This was the opportunity to find out more about our victim. Okay, Mark and D hadn't thought about it either, so maybe stupid was a little harsh. Time to change that. "Was that a problem sometimes? Her passion?"

"Oh, you know how it is. Some people prefer the path of least resistance, but Amalia would dig in her heels when she thought something was important." Margaret's expression grew more serious. "She'd been particularly concerned lately about some of the methods being used by various councils. Said there were too many people more interested in control than protection."

"Amalia could be stubborn as a mule," said another voice behind me. I turned to see a man in his forties with paint-stained fingers extending his hand. "David Morse. I ran an arts collective with Amalia in Seattle."

"Stubborn about what?" I asked.

"About doing things the right way, even when the right way was harder," David said. "She spent six months fighting our council about a rule they wanted to install—to keep us from interacting with plain humans in any circumstance. Wouldn't give up until they agreed to back off. I loved her for it, most of us did. If no plain humans could shop at our galleries or restaurants? We'd lose our biggest revenue stream."

While David told his story, I caught sight of a witch who must be Beatrix across the lobby. She was talking quietly with Helena, and both women kept glancing in my direction. When they noticed me watching, they separated quickly.

I made my way over to D, who was talking to the bus driver. A plain human, but I shouldn't be surprised. There were only so many services witches could offer. And David's comments rose in my memory. If the council had succeeded, isolation would have made things much worse.

"Any useful information?" I asked quietly as we walked away.

"The driver confirmed they're all planning to go back to Vancouver and Seattle tonight after the ceremony," D said. "Memorial at sunset, then the bus leaves around nine PM. So this really is just a day trip for them."

"What about Beatrix? I saw her—at least someone who matched the description. Did you see when she arrived?"

"Yes, she's here. She was already here when the bus pulled up. Must have driven herself." D lowered his voice. "And she's been having a lot of quiet conversations with Helena. More than you'd expect if she just got back from investigating tea sources."

That was interesting. If Beatrix had finished her investigation, why wasn't she reporting to the full council? And why didn't I know her results?

I continued mingling and talked to a younger woman named Michelle Varmer who'd driven up from Portland to catch the bus in Seattle.

"Amalia could be exhausting to work with sometimes," Michelle said when I asked about her memories. "But she was always fighting for the people who couldn't fight for themselves. Families, kids, anyone the councils wanted to treat as a problem to be solved rather than people to be helped."

"I think that's the main reason the council came up here," I said. "To find a common ground."

"She didn't tell me," Michelle said. "We talked a little over the last few months. She'd been increasingly frustrated with some of the Vancouver council's policies. Said they were becoming too authoritarian and needed to be reminded that they serve the community, not the other way around."

As I wandered around the group, I kept my eyes on Maria and Beatrix. Maria's emotions leaked a little with genuine grief. Was that proof she hadn't killed the woman? Beatrix was the opposite. She didn't initiate any conversations, and few people approached her. The only emotion I could access was serenity. It felt completely wrong in the circumstances.

"This feels surreal," I said to Mark when he joined me near the windows. "One of these people probably killed Amalia, and now they're all helping organize her memorial."

"We'll figure it out," Mark said quietly. "Don't we just have three suspects? Maria with her earring evidence, Helena with her pattern of lies, or Beatrix with her convenient absences and mysterious investigations."

"Yes, for now. It could be someone we haven't even considered yet," I said, watching as the three women continued to interact with Amalia's friends and colleagues.

30

As afternoon turned toward evening, Helena began organizing everyone for the move to the forest clearing. I watched the logistics with growing unease—thirty grieving witches, plus the Vancouver council, including one murderer. It occurred to me that maybe this whole event was called to distract us from the murder. Surely none of the council would be able to break their oath to stay.

"Ms. Fortuna," Helena said, approaching me with a clipboard and speaking loud enough for Toni behind the reception counter to hear. "We could use your help coordinating the transition to the outdoor portion of our... celebration."

The way she said "celebration" while her eyes conveyed the gravity of moving a body made me realize how precarious this whole situation was.

"What do you need me to do?" I asked, playing along.

"Help manage the flow of people," she said, lowering her voice to almost a whisper. "We need to get everyone to the clearing without suspicion from the hotel staff, and we need to transport Amalia without anyone noticing."

I glanced around the lobby. The memorial guests were chatting in small groups, but I could see hotel employees moving through the area, offering assistance and clearly curious about the large group.

"How exactly are we moving... her?" I asked quietly.

"James has a concealment spell prepared. To anyone mundane, it will look like we're carrying equipment for a nature meditation session." Helena checked her clipboard. "But we need people moving in smaller groups so it doesn't look like a procession."

I started helping organize people into groups of four and five, directing them toward the forest path at staggered intervals. As I worked, I caught fragments of conversations that made me pay closer attention.

"...Amalia was right about the Vancouver approach being too heavy-handed," a woman named Linda was saying to her companion. "But I'm not sure her methods would have worked either. That was something she always missed."

"The Seattle community has been watching the Vancouver situation with interest," replied an older man I'd heard introduced as Thomas. "Some of us think Amalia's collaborative model is exactly what we need."

"And others think it's dangerously naive," another woman said with a meaningful look.

I helped direct their group toward the forest while processing what I'd heard. It sounded like there were philosophical divisions even among Amalia's supporters.

I was learning so much about Amalia, but it wasn't helping to find the killer.

"I still can't believe Amalia would give up the fight," said Margaret Simmons, the woman I'd spoken to earlier. "She was so passionate about reforming council practices. It doesn't seem like her to just... stop."

Her companion, David Morse, lowered his voice. "Patricia thinks there's more to the story. She said Amalia had been working on something important, some kind of proposal that she was going to send to the other councils in the area. Get some allies before going to Mrs. Vestum."

"What kind of proposal?" Margaret asked.

I wanted to know too. This could be our motive! I had no idea if it was normal to shop a proposal around or to bring in the protector.

"Standards for training. Some ideas for setting up remote centers for kids who need protection while they learn—places for their families to stay and more experienced witches to act as teachers. I mean, it sounds great, but as far as I know, there isn't a rash of erratic magic happening."

"Cossi?" D appeared at my elbow. "Helena wants us to help with the... equipment transport."

I followed him to a service corridor where James O'Brien was standing with what looked like several pieces of meditation equipment—folded mats, cushions, and a small altar. But I could sense the concealment spell shimmering around the items, and I realized one of the "bundles" was Amalia's body.

"Everyone ready?" James asked quietly.

Mark, D, and I each took some of the actual equipment while James and Robert Kim carefully lifted the concealed bundle. To anyone watching, we looked like volunteers helping set up for an outdoor corporate team-building activity.

As we walked through the lobby and out toward the forest path, I heard one of the hotel staff comment to another, "These meditation companies sure take their retreats seriously. All that equipment for one evening session."

The concealment spell was working perfectly.

The forest path was beautiful in the early evening light, and I could see why the council had chosen this location. The clearing was far enough from the hotel to provide privacy, but not so far that older guests would have trouble with the walk.

As we reached the clearing, I noticed that people were naturally separating into two distinct groups, though they were still talking across the divide. It wasn't obvious—both groups were setting up chairs and helping arrange the space —but there was definitely a subtle separation.

"I am observing the same phenomenon," Destroyer observed. I glanced up and saw him perched on a branch.

"Aren't you usually sleeping by now?"

"I find myself interested in the funeral customs of humans. I want to know how different they are from crow rites."

I'd done my research, so I wasn't surprised by the funeral thing. "Why would you need to know that?"

"When I expand my empire beyond the animals of the sky and land, I will need to be prepared."

I stifled the inappropriate laugh. "A long time from now, I hope. Keep your eyes on the crowd. I hope someone will make a mistake."

James and Robert carefully placed Amalia's body in the prepared area—still concealed but now positioned for the ceremony. I was able to focus on the people around me.

"...Helena's been very gracious making all the arrangements," someone was saying, "but I know she and Amalia had their differences about protocol."

"Didn't we all?"

"Helena believes in following established procedures, even when they're harsh. Amalia thought procedures should serve people, not the other way around." I didn't know the witches involved in the conversation, but this wasn't news, so I didn't introduce myself.

I looked across the clearing at Helena, who was efficiently directing the final setup. She caught my eye and nodded professionally, but I found myself wondering what other "differences" she and Amalia might have had.

A reason to think we should dig deeper into Helena's motives? I stored the comment away.

As the sun began to set and the memorial service prepared to begin, I realized that we weren't just here to say goodbye to Amalia Svoboda. We were witnessing the intersection of all the conflicts and tensions that had led to her death.

31

As the memorial service began, I positioned myself where I could observe both the ceremony and the group dynamics. What I saw confirmed my earlier suspicions—while everyone was here to honor Amalia, there were definitely two distinct factions represented.

Elizabeth Morrison stepped forward to begin the service, her voice carrying clearly across the clearing. "We gather tonight to celebrate the life and work of Amalia Svoboda, a colleague whose passion for justice touched us all."

The responses highlighted the difference between the groups. Most of the crowd murmured a gentle agreement, but a few didn't respond at all.

"Amalia believed deeply in the power of collaboration," Elizabeth continued. "She worked tirelessly to find solutions that honored both community security and individual dignity. I'll let others talk about their memories of her now."

Margaret Simmons was the first to speak, stepping

forward from what I was beginning to think of as the collaborative side of the gathering.

"Amalia never accepted 'that's how we've always done it' as an answer," Margaret said, her voice warm with affection. "She'd spend hours researching alternatives, talking to everyone, finding creative solutions that protected everyone involved. It didn't matter to her if the issue was large or small."

David Morse spoke next. "I know some of her friends often found her frustrating as she worked through her process. I won't mention names, but you know who you are." Chuckles rippled through the crowd.

"That's exactly the kind of innovation we need more of," another witch called out.

The older man I'd overheard earlier stood up with a more measured response. "Amalia's heart was always in the right place," he said carefully. "But sometimes her optimism about what was possible led her to underestimate real dangers. I don't know if she even realized how important it is to let others feel heard."

The collaborative faction shifted uncomfortably, but no one contradicted him directly. I wondered if a memorial was usually an opportunity to analyze the deceased's personality. I glanced over to Mark and D, who stood a little into the trees. No reaction I could read, so maybe this was normal.

Helena spoke next, and I listened carefully to her words. "Amalia brought a fresh perspective to difficult decisions. She challenged us to think beyond our first instincts and consider long-term consequences."

It was a diplomatic statement that could appeal to both sides, but I noticed that Helena's tone was more formal than genuinely warm. I'm not sure what I expected to learn, but nothing so far pointed to a suspect.

As more people shared memories, the philosophical divide became clearer without ever being explicitly stated. One group emphasized Amalia's advocacy for families and individuals facing council decisions. They talked about her willingness to fight authority when she thought policies were wrong. I was heartened that she wasn't the only voice of what I thought was reason.

The other group, while respectful, focused more on Amalia's dedication to community welfare and her understanding of security challenges. They praised her thoroughness and her commitment to finding solutions that worked for everyone.

"She could be stubborn," admitted Robert Kim, speaking for the first time. "When Amalia thought something was unjust, she wouldn't let it go. Sometimes that made things... difficult."

"Difficult for stick-in-the-muds," a male witch across from him said.

Robert glanced toward Maria, who was sitting quietly in the middle ground between the two factions. "She didn't always understand that compromise is sometimes necessary. That protecting the community as a whole might require difficult decisions about individuals."

"Or maybe," said a voice from the collaborative side, "she understood that protecting individuals is protecting the community."

I noticed that Maria winced slightly at that exchange, as if it touched on something painful. I prepared myself for a— well, not a fight, but this wasn't a place to hash out grievances.

As the testimonials continued, I began to understand the real conflict that had driven Amalia's work—and possibly her death. It wasn't just about the Reeves family or even about the Vancouver council specifically. It was about two fundamentally different approaches to magical community governance.

One side believed that security came through strong controls, clear hierarchies, and sometimes hard choices about who to protect first. The other believed that security came through inclusion, collaboration, and refusing to sacrifice individuals for abstract concepts of community welfare. There didn't seem to be any official stance on the subject.

Both sides loved Amalia, but for different reasons. The collaborators saw her as a champion of their values. The security-focused group saw her as someone whose heart was in the right place but whose methods were dangerously idealistic. And no one was radiating any fury, remorse, or any other emotion that helped me pin them down.

"She was working on something important before she..." a witch said and then paused, clearly catching herself before mentioning death. "Before she got sick. A recommendation for standardizing council behavior."

"What kind of standardization, Patricia?" Helena asked, and I heard a note of tension in her voice. "We should have been made aware."

"Documentation of cases where reactions had been unnecessarily harsh. A comparison of outcomes from councils with different approaches," Patricia explained. "She was planning to present it to the regional council coordination meeting next month."

The security-focused faction exchanged glances. I could sense their discomfort with the idea of formal criticism of council policies. And I think Helena had a point. From my perspective, not informing her peers made Amalia look... scheming?

Maria finally spoke, her voice quiet but carrying across the clearing. "Amalia believed that our fear was making us forget our values. She thought we were becoming too much like the things we were trying to protect ourselves from. But this is not the forum for picking over her choices."

"I think it would be good to discuss these ideas another time," I said, trying to stave off the complaint session that was building steam. "We should continue to honor Amalia."

Whether it was because I was the protector or because everyone realized they'd strayed off the subject, the speakers returned to sharing memories and stories about Amalia.

By the time the ceremony was winding down, I had a much better picture of her. Yes, passionate and stubborn, which could be good and bad, but also fun and smart. Everyone here, including the killer, would miss her.

32

As the memorial service concluded and we approached the burial, a few people made their way back toward the hotel. I felt overwhelmed by everything I'd observed. This was a much more complicated case than I was used to solving. I never wanted to be good at this. The magical world should be better than the plain one, right? No. People are people. I needed to get over my expectations and see the reality.

"You look troubled," Mark said quietly as two of the witches cast spells to create a grave.

"No kidding," I admitted. "This isn't just about one person killing another. This is about fundamental disagreements over how magical communities should operate. Even when we find the killer, there's going to be a lot of work to stop the councils from drifting to the extremes."

"A strong leader holds a firm leash," Destroyer pontificated. "Do not be distracted by future tasks."

"If I don't think about the future, I'll make it worse."

"Your mentor will help," he said. "I must now go and prepare my new realm to continue in my absence."

New realm? I really needed to have a long conversation with Destroyer about respecting boundaries. I told D and Mark what Destroyer said.

"Maybe he's right," D suggested, folding up the last of the meditation mats. "I mean, not completely—he's a bit of a nutcase—but if you try to solve the future when you've got a specific problem, you'll never get anywhere."

"But that's just it," I said, my frustration spilling over. "From what I heard tonight, lots of people felt challenged by Amalia's approach. The entire security-focused faction thought her methods were dangerous. Any of them could have felt threatened enough to act. My power is telling me that's the motive for the murder. If I ignore it, we'll just keep coming back to solve more problems."

"You are overthinking again," Destroyer said despite saying he was going. "The emperor does not concern himself with every possible motivation. He focuses on the evidence that points to specific individuals."

"What evidence?" I asked aloud. "An earring that could have been planted? Witness testimony about midnight pacing that could have innocent explanations? Lies from Helena that might be about protecting the council's reputation rather than covering up murder?"

"You sound like you're losing confidence," Mark said, studying my expression with concern.

"Maybe I am," I said. "What if we're wrong about everything? What if Maria really is innocent and we're about to destroy her life? What if the real killer is someone we haven't even considered seriously?"

D put his hand on my shoulder and reassurance flowed into me. "Cossi, you've been protector for less than a week. You solved multiple murders on Henbane before that happened. You have good instincts. We find the killer and everything after that is a different project."

If only it were that easy. I agreed with all of the logic. The niggling voice in my head told me I was still as much in the dark about being the protector as I'd been when I arrived on Henbane about being a witch.

"By remembering that you can get help on the bigger issue," Mark said firmly. "You are not the only protector. Your job is to find out who killed Amalia Svoboda. Everything else is context."

The remaining witches were almost ready for the burial by now. Another ceremony I didn't know. Was I expected to cast some kind of spell?

"You know what I think?" D said after a moment. "I think you're getting caught up in the complexity because you're afraid of being wrong. But remember, the protector can't be wrong."

"I'll try, but since I've never seen it in action, I don't know. My instincts are telling me the motive isn't what we think," I said. "It's more complicated."

"Then trust that," Mark said. "You knew what to do for the Reeves—you'll know what to do here."

The burial itself was surprisingly peaceful. As the memorial guests gathered in a circle around the prepared site, James removed the concealment spell with a gentle gesture. For the first time tonight, I could see Amalia clearly. Lying down made her look like she was simply sleeping, which somehow made the whole ceremony feel more like a proper farewell.

"Does anyone have final words they'd like to share?" Elizabeth asked softly.

Helena stepped forward. "Amalia always said that the best way to honor someone's memory was to continue their work. I hope we can all find ways to do that, even when we disagree about methods."

There were murmurs of agreement from both factions, and I found myself thinking that maybe these philosophical differences didn't have to be so divisive after all.

Ormand placed a small bouquet of wildflowers on the grave. "She would have loved being buried here," he said. "Amalia always felt more at peace in nature than in boardrooms."

"She did love the outdoors," Helena agreed, and for the first time since we'd arrived, her professional composure seemed to crack slightly. "She used to say that spending time in forests helped her remember what we were really trying to protect."

Earth slid in to fill the hole and I felt a weight lift. One danger averted. No plain humans had discovered the truth, and now they wouldn't. I didn't even know I was worried about that, but suddenly things didn't seem so complicated. It was like someone had lifted a confusion spell. I didn't think the protector could be affected like that, but then, I didn't really know enough about the role.

33

When the ground looked undisturbed, we drifted back to the lodge. The memorial guests would be leaving soon, returning to their own communities and their own versions of the conflicts we'd witnessed tonight.

"Let's meet in an hour," I said to Mark and D as we neared the lodge. "After everyone's gone. I want to talk through what we've learned and figure out what it means for our investigation. I want this solved by tomorrow." Only because it was getting too late to say today.

"Good idea," Mark agreed. "We learned a lot about her, and talking through the evidence through a new lens may help clarify things."

"And Cossi?" D added. "Remember that you don't have to solve this alone. We're here to help, and Mrs. V is just a phone call away if you need guidance."

As I watched the memorial guests say their goodbyes and gather their belongings, I tried to organize my thoughts. D was right that I was getting caught up in the complexity, but I couldn't shake the feeling that the complexity was important.

Amalia hadn't been killed in a moment of passion or by a stranger looking for easy money. She'd been killed by someone who knew her well enough to get into her room, who understood her habits enough to use tea as a weapon, and who felt strongly enough about her work to choose murder over continued opposition.

"The philosophical divide isn't just background," I said to Destroyer as I watched the bus pull away. "It's the key to understanding why someone thought killing Amalia was worth the risk."

"Then use that understanding," he replied. "But remember that emperors act based on evidence, not endless contemplation."

With that statement, it was clear he didn't know the history of monarchs. "You're right," I said, feeling my confidence starting to return. "It's time to stop second-guessing myself and start acting on what we know."

I wanted to stay outside while I thought, so I followed a trail to a bench and sat. I made a mental list of what we needed to discuss: the earring evidence, the witness testimony, the pattern of lies from various council members, and most importantly, the motive that was becoming clearer with each conversation.

Someone at this memorial had killed Amalia Svoboda because they believed her approach to community governance was too dangerous to continue—I was certain of that, but couldn't explain it beyond the fact that my power told me so. Now I just had to figure out which person had been willing to commit murder to stop her. And despite my earlier doubts, I was starting to think I knew exactly who that person was.

"I shall establish a proper honor guard for her resting place," Destroyer announced, fluttering down to perch on my shoulder. I tried not to wince as his talons pierced my skin again. "For three days, or until you all go home."

"That's very thoughtful," I said, meaning it. "Thank you."

"Great leaders understand the importance of proper ceremonial respect," he replied with dignity. "Even those who were not privileged to serve under my command deserve honor in death."

The visiting witches were gathering at the bus when I came back to the lodge. I caught a few scraps of conversation and paused to hear more.

"...such a relief to finally have closure," someone was saying. "This whole situation has been so stressful for everyone."

"Helena's handled the arrangements beautifully," came a reply. "Though I know this has been hard on her personally."

Behind me, I heard Robert Kim talking quietly to James O'Brien. "I'm just glad we can all go home tomorrow and try to move forward."

"Do you think things will change now?" James asked.

"They'll have to. Amalia's death—even from natural causes—is going to raise questions about work-life balance in council positions."

I found it interesting that even among themselves, they were maintaining the natural causes story. The cover-up had been thorough.

By the time I reached the entrance, most of the memorial guests were already boarding the bus for their return journey. I watched through the lobby windows as they said their final goodbyes, hugging each other to help ease their shared grief.

As the bus pulled away into the night, I noticed Maria and Beatrix having what looked like an intense quiet conversation near the elevators. Both women kept glancing around to see if anyone was watching, and when Helena approached them, Beatrix quickly walked away toward the front desk. I still hadn't talked to her, but this wasn't the time.

"Everything all right?" I heard Helena ask Maria.

"Just tired," Maria replied, but I could sense tension in her voice that hadn't been there during the ceremony.

A few minutes later, I saw Beatrix and Helena having their own quiet discussion near the hotel entrance. Helena looked agitated, gesturing emphatically while Beatrix remained calm and controlled. When they noticed me watching, they separated immediately.

"Well," Elizabeth said with a sigh as the lobby finally quieted, "I suppose we should make arrangements to check out tomorrow morning. There's no reason to extend our stay now that the memorial is complete."

I checked with my power, deciding to be more in tune with it, to see if I needed to make them stay another night, but there was nothing.

"The hotel has been very accommodating," Helena added, back to her professional manner. "We should express our appreciation for their help in extending our stay."

As people dispersed to their rooms for the evening, I felt a mixture of relief and anticipation. The memorial was over, Amalia was properly buried, and the concealment spells were no longer straining the magical environment. Now we could focus entirely on the investigation without worrying about magical exposure or managing additional people.

But I couldn't shake the feeling that something important had happened in those brief conversations between the council members. The way Beatrix had quickly walked away when Helena approached, and the tension I'd sensed from Maria, suggested that not everyone was ready to simply go home and move on.

"Did you notice the body language during those conversations?" D asked quietly as he and Mark joined me in the lobby.

"I did," I said. "It looked like disagreements about something, but they were trying to keep it private."

"Maybe about how to handle things now that the memorial is over?" Mark suggested.

"Maybe," I said, but I suspected it was more significant than that. "I think we need to pay closer attention to the remaining council members tonight. Something feels unresolved. And I don't want any of them testing my order to stay."

"Good point," Mark agreed. "And Cossi? I want to make sure you know that you handled today really well. We talked a lot about how hard this is, but you are doing the right things."

We headed to my room to hash through the new perspective, but after a few minutes, Mark and D left. We needed to sleep more than to just keep going over the same clues.

34

The next morning, Mark, D, and I gathered in the small conference room with coffee and notebooks, refreshed and ready to work through everything we'd learned.

"Elizabeth was absolutely right," I said as I settled into my chair. "Having the body hidden and all those people to manage was making it impossible to think clearly. Now we can actually focus on the investigation."

"Where do you want to start?" Mark asked, pen poised over his notepad.

"With motives," I said. "We keep getting distracted by the evidence, but what I observed at the memorial service made it clear that the real key is understanding why someone would kill Amalia."

D pulled out his tablet and created a new document. "Let's list all the possible motives we've considered."

"Professional jealousy," I started. "Helena feeling threatened by Amalia's criticism of her methods."

"Personal conflict," Mark added. "Maria and Amalia's ongoing arguments about community governance."

"Fear of exposure," D said. "Someone worried that Amalia's documentation project would reveal inappropriate council actions."

"Power struggle," I continued. "Someone who saw Amalia's collaborative approach as a threat to established authority."

"Revenge," Mark suggested. "Though we haven't found evidence of anyone having a personal grudge against Amalia."

"I can provide assistance with some of these theories," Destroyer announced from a perch outside. I wished I could bring him inside, but the windows didn't open. "I have recruited local mice to observe the remaining council members."

"What kind of observations?" I asked after passing on his comments.

"Behavioral patterns, emotional states, private conversations when they think no one is listening. My language skills are excellent," he stated. "Mice are tasty, I hear, but they are also capable agents."

I had to smile at the idea of tiny surveillance operatives. "What have they learned?"

"Several interesting details. The silver-haired witch has been crying alone in her room each evening since the memorial. She speaks aloud to herself about 'terrible mistakes' and 'things that can't be undone.'"

That could be evidence of guilt, or it could just be grief over losing a colleague she'd argued with. I translated his report.

"What about Helena?" Mark asked. "Or Beatrix? Or what the heck these mistakes are?"

I wished we'd thought to ask Destroyer to spy on all of our suspects.

"The one named Helena is methodical in her behaviors but shows signs of stress. She makes many phone calls about damage control and maintaining community stability. However, she does not cry or show that she is sad."

"That sounds like Helena is focusing on practical concerns rather than grief," D observed when I told them.

"I wonder if her stress is about anything particular," I said, "or general stress about council decisions?"

"And the formal witch—Elizabeth—maintains rigid control during the day, but my operatives have observed her throwing objects in her room when she thinks no one can hear. The new witch—I believe this is Beatrix—sleeps soundly."

I looked at Mark and D. "So we have Maria crying about mistakes, Helena focused on damage control, and Elizabeth having private meltdowns. If Beatrix is sleeping well, perhaps we'll put her at the bottom of our list of suspects."

"That eliminates some motives," Mark said thoughtfully. "If Maria is genuinely grieving and feeling guilty, it's less likely she killed Amalia at all, let alone out of professional jealousy or power struggles."

"Unless the guilt is because she committed murder," D pointed out.

"But would someone who killed for calculated reasons be crying about mistakes?" I asked. "That sounds more like someone who argued with a friend and then lost them before they could reconcile."

"The Helena behaviors are interesting too," Mark said. "Focusing on damage control could mean she's covering up a crime, or it could mean she's genuinely trying to protect the community from scandal."

I thought about what we'd observed during the memorial service. "You know what struck me yesterday? Both

Maria and Helena seemed genuinely affected by Amalia's death, but in different ways."

"How so?"

"Maria looked like she was grieving someone she'd cared about but disagreed with. Helena looked like she was managing a professional crisis while also dealing with personal loss. Neither oozed guilt or remorse."

"I kind of noticed that too. So what does that tell us about motives?" D asked.

"Maybe we need to focus on which motives would drive someone to actual murder," I said slowly. "Professional disagreements, even heated ones, don't usually lead to killing." Like I was the expert.

"What does lead to murder?" Mark asked. "We only have what drove the ones on Henbane to learn from. I don't think watching mysteries or reading gives us real experience."

Yes, fiction was all managed toward an end. Reality was far more chaotic. "Fear," I said, "that something you care deeply about is under threat. Or that someone is going to destroy something you've worked your whole life to build."

"Or ideology," D added. "When someone believes so strongly in their approach that they see opposition as genuinely dangerous."

"Those are the only two motives that make sense for this crime," I said as the realization filled me. "Either someone was afraid that Amalia's project would destroy them personally, or someone believed so strongly that her collaborative approach was dangerous that they thought killing her was justified. I've been complicating this by dithering."

"Not dithering," Mark said. "We were gathering data. So which council members fit those profiles?"

"Helena could fit the fear motive if she was involved in council decisions that Amalia was documenting," I said. "But the fear would have to be about more than just professional embarrassment. It would have to be fear of genuine consequences. I wonder if someone made a mistake in their past —something no one knows about?"

"And Maria could fit the ideological motive," D said. "She really believes that rules need to be enforced."

"But here's what I don't understand," I said. "Both Helena and Maria were the ones who suggested hiding the body and calling for a protector. Why would the killer propose bringing in an investigator? Why not just bury the body and cast a spell to make people forget?"

"Maybe because they thought they could control the investigation," Mark suggested. "Or maybe because not calling for help would have looked suspicious."

"Or maybe," I said slowly, "because one of them is innocent and genuinely wanted help, while the other is guilty and thought they could misdirect the investigation."

The room went quiet as we all considered that possibility.

I flushed as my power confirmed I was on the right track.

35

A fter breakfast I wandered to the lobby thinking about my next steps. We couldn't let this investigation drag on. Our meeting earlier had narrowed down the suspects to Helena and Maria. If one of those two hadn't committed the crime, then I didn't know how to restart. Trust my power was easy to say, but without any real experience, how did I know I understood what it told me?

Elizabeth was talking to Toni at the reception desk. I heard the words "check out time" and headed over to find out what she was planning.

"Cossi," Elizabeth said when I joined them, "we're planning to leave this afternoon. Will that give you enough time to complete your follow-up questions?" She raised an eyebrow. Oh, she wanted to know if I'd lift the stay-put order.

Did she forget we hadn't solved the murder? "What time is check-out?" I didn't want to talk in front of Toni, so I drew Elizabeth away.

"I've arranged for a late one," she said. "Four o'clock. It gives you time to wrap up loose ends."

"Tell her you will decide when they can leave," Destroyer said. "I wish to return to Henbane, but burying the body is insufficient. An emperor does not dance to the tune of their subjects."

That was not helping. I told him to let me think. We couldn't just keep extending the stay, and I only had two suspects. "That should be fine," I said to Elizabeth. "I'll join the council soon. We believe we know the culprit."

My brainstorm, if you could call it that, was to stir things up. Elizabeth would pass on the information to the other council members. The killer should react.

"We're having a final meeting in the large conference room," she said. "Our original purpose was not resolved. Perhaps without Maria and Amalia's passion, logic will get us to a solution."

Even better. Everyone in one place was going to make this faster. I ordered a coffee from the café and took it outside. Mark and D were researching every council member to prove our theory. Time to learn what Destroyer's spy network had uncovered.

"Do you have any news to help?" I asked quietly. Talking aloud to my familiar helped, but I rarely got the opportunity outside Henbane.

"The Maria witch spent much of the night pacing and speaking to herself about protecting the community and making hard choices. A good habit for a leader to think that way."

"How do you know all this?" It's not like he could read.

"I am the emperor of the world. I know how to behave and understand what is needed."

"You know I can tell you lied, right?" My mood was lifting already.

"I am also able to see and hear what witches think of as entertainment. I have learned much from programs about human history." He kind of huffed out the words.

I hoped he didn't mean Game of Thrones. Or, come to think of it, any real history. Although perhaps knowing what happened to despots would keep him from becoming one. "We'll talk more about this when we're home. Is there anything else?"

"My spies report she seemed to be practicing speeches of some kind. Pacing, talking, repeating herself."

Practicing for the last meeting, or her confession?

"What about Helena?"

"She made numerous communications with various councils, consistently using phrases about maintaining stability and preventing widespread panic. She appears focused on coordinating responses to what she terms political consequences."

Interesting. Either Helena was covering up her own crime, or she was genuinely trying to manage a crisis that someone else had created.

"And Beatrix? The witch who was not here most of the time."

"Ah, the intelligence officer presents the most intriguing behaviors," Destroyer said. I might not be able to see him, but the preening was clear in his tone. "She has engaged in multiple urgent consultations with all other witches, but separately. My network indicates significant disagreement about proper protocols."

"What kind of disagreements?" I said and then jumped as Mark and D joined me on the bench.

"I think I need to interview three witches separately to

find out," I said to Mark and D. "Mice can only do so much. We need to be careful, though. If one of them is the killer, I don't want to spook them into running or doing something desperate." I thanked Destroyer and turned his attention to imperial matters.

"Who do you want to start with?" Mark asked. "You mean Helena, Maria, and I think Beatrix? We haven't talked to her yet."

Before I could answer, Robert Kim approached us looking nervous. "Ms. Fortuna, could I speak with you privately? There's something I think you should know."

"You can talk to all of us," I said, not willing to be alone with any of the council members in this isolated part of the woods.

"Very well. It's about the night Amalia died," he said quietly. "I didn't mention this before because I wasn't sure it was relevant, but after everything that's happened..."

No more waffling. "What did you see?"

"I told you I heard footsteps in the hallway around midnight, but I didn't mention that I also heard voices. Two people having a very quiet conversation outside my door."

The conversation or argument we knew about. Perhaps he had some details. "Could you make out any words?"

"Just fragments. Someone said 'we have to call for help' and 'this can't be covered up.' Then the other person said something about 'making things worse' and 'handling it ourselves.'"

My heart started beating faster. That was definitely a huge clue. "Could you identify the voices?"

"One was definitely Beatrix. I've heard her give enough reports to recognize her voice even when she's whispering." Robert paused. "The other... I'm not entirely sure, but I think it might have been Maria. She was the one saying things about making it worse."

"You think Beatrix and Maria were arguing about what happened?" D and Mark sat still as if trying to disappear.

"It sounded like they disagreed about what to do after... after whatever had happened to Amalia. Like they were debating whether to call for outside help or try to handle the situation internally."

I thanked Robert and asked him to give us time to think.

When he was gone, D said, "So Beatrix and Maria were arguing about whether to call for a protector."

"That actually makes sense if we're right," Mark added. "Amalia had just died under suspicious circumstances—the council should have reached out to you immediately. The killer would want to hide the evidence, not call for an investigation."

"And we know from Helena's behavior that she was the one who ultimately made the call to Mrs. V," I said. "So maybe Maria wanted to handle it internally, Beatrix disagreed, and Helena made the final decision."

"But that still doesn't tell us who actually killed Amalia," D pointed out. "Just because Beatrix and Helena wanted to call you in doesn't make them innocent."

"No, but it tells us something important about the aftermath," I said slowly. "If Beatrix was arguing for calling in help immediately, she's probably not the killer. Someone who committed murder wouldn't want external investigators involved or wouldn't have had any time to cover evidence."

"And if Maria was arguing against calling for help..." Mark said.

"Then she might have been trying to buy time to cover her tracks," I finished. "Or she might have been genuinely worried about scandal affecting the community, or the effect of an investigation in the midst of plain humans."

We let that sit for a few minutes as I dug in my mind for a plan. "We need to interview Maria directly. If she's been practicing speeches about hard choices and protecting the community, and if she was arguing against calling for help, she might be ready to tell us what really happened."

"Are you prepared for a confession?" Mark asked. "If that's what happens?"

I thought about everything we'd learned. Nothing had pointed directly at Maria until now. "I think so," I said. "But I want to approach it carefully. If Maria really believes she was protecting the community, she might be more willing to explain her actions than to simply admit guilt."

36

I wasn't ready to confront Maria without checking on the other suspect. Yes, I knew both of them had motive, but my power told me that Helena would be reasonable—maybe because everything we knew about Maria screamed that she was about to explode, even if she was innocent.

We found Helena in the small conference room, her phone on the table and pads of paper arranged around her. The picture of an executive in full planning mode. How could she return to business so easily? Was burial some kind of checkpoint for emotions in a witch?

"Helena," I said, settling into the chair across from her while D and Mark stood behind me, "we need to talk about what really happened the night Amalia died."

She pushed her phone a little farther away and faced me, her expression carefully neutral. "I've told you everything I know about that night. I can't believe you think I held anything back."

"Have you?" Mark asked, pulling out his notebook. "Because we've learned some things that suggest the story is more complicated than you initially indicated. In fact, you held back a lot, right?"

Helena's emotional state shifted slightly—not guilt, but wariness mixed with resignation—then her shield snapped into place. "What exactly are you asking me?"

"We know you've been managing damage control since Amalia's death," I said. "We know you were involved in the decision to conceal her body and call for a protector. What we want to know is whether you were involved in her death itself." I figured it was time to be blunt. If she lied now, both Mark and I would know.

Helena was quiet for a long moment, and I could sense her weighing what she could get away with keeping secret. "I didn't kill Amalia," she said finally. "But I did help cover it up afterward."

Cover it up? Very different from protecting the scene.

"Why?" D asked.

"Because I thought it was the best solution for everyone involved." Helena's professional composure cracked slightly. "When I found out what had happened, my first instinct was to protect the community from scandal. Calling attention to a murder within the council would have damaged the trust people have in the council. When you're at risk of discovery every moment, you learn to avoid any hint of something different."

That was a huge exaggeration. I'd lived as a plain human. They weren't looking for some kind of hidden magical world—well, some conspiracy nuts were always looking for something like that, but living under constant fear was something this council had created.

"So you knew it was murder from the beginning?" Mark asked. He wasn't letting her distract him from the topic.

"I suspected. When Maria came to me that night, she was... distraught. She said Amalia was dead and that we needed to handle the situation carefully. She suggested we treat it as a natural death and avoid involving outside authorities."

"And you agreed?" I asked. "You thought there was a killer among you and thought the best thing was to pretend everything was okay?"

"Initially, yes. But of course, as I thought about it more, I realized that a cover-up would only make things worse if the truth came out later. Beatrix helped me think rationally when I talked to her. That's when we decided to call you, Cossi."

She let her shields down, and I studied Helena's emotions carefully. Relief at finally telling the truth, guilt about the cover-up, but no deception about her role in the actual murder.

"Helena," I said gently, "I need you to be completely honest. Did you have any role in Amalia's death beyond helping to conceal it afterward?"

"No," she said firmly. "I disagreed with many of Amalia's approaches, but I would never have hurt her. She was a colleague and, despite our differences, someone I respected."

Mark looked up from his notes. "She's telling the truth," he said.

I felt a mixture of relief and frustration. Relief that we'd eliminated one suspect, but frustration that we were back to having limited options. Or maybe it was all relief. In one sentence, Helena had cleared both Beatrix and herself. I was right. Maria was our killer.

"Where is Maria now?" I asked.

"In her room, I assume," Helena said. "She's been

avoiding us since... well, you know. The others think she's grieving. I'm not so sure."

"We need to talk to her," I said, standing up. "Helena, I'd like you to come with us."

She straightened, and a spike of shock ran through her emotions. "Why?"

"Because if Maria is our killer, having you there might help convince her to tell us the truth," I said. Helena was a familiar face, and I hoped it would keep Maria calm.

We made our way up to Maria's room, but when Helena knocked, there was no answer.

"Maria?" Helena called. "It's Helena. We need to talk."

Still no response. Helena pulled a handful of keycards from her pocket and tried them until the door unlocked. "I have copies of everyone's." She didn't add any details about why.

The room was empty, but Maria's belongings were still scattered around—clothes folded on the chair, toiletries on the bathroom counter, her suitcase open on the luggage rack. It didn't look like she was getting ready to pack and go home.

"She's here somewhere. Maria wouldn't have left without her things," Helena said, looking puzzled.

"Unless she left in a hurry," Mark pointed out. "If she didn't think she had time."

I walked to the window and looked out at the parking area. "Her car is still here too."

D glanced into the bathroom. "We saw her after the bus left, so she's still close."

Helena sank into the chair by the window. "I should have seen this coming. Maria has been struggling with guilt since Amalia's death. She kept saying that she'd made a terrible mistake, that she'd acted out of fear rather than wisdom. How could I have missed this?"

Only she could answer that question. "Fear of what?" I asked, hoping it was something to help find her.

"Fear that Amalia's project would destroy everything our councils have built," she said to herself more than to me. "Maria genuinely believed that exposing our methods to that kind of scrutiny would lead to community chaos and exposure to the mundane world."

"So she thought killing Amalia was justified?" Mark asked.

"I think she convinced herself it was necessary," Helena said sadly. "But the guilt has been eating her alive ever since. She's not a bad person."

I looked around the abandoned room, trying to think like someone who was running scared but couldn't actually leave. "She's still here somewhere," I said. "The question is where, and whether she's planning to turn herself in or try to disappear permanently."

"Could she try to leave on foot?" D asked, but even he didn't think so.

"Maybe, but Manning Park is pretty isolated. She wouldn't get far without a vehicle," Helena said.

"We need to find her before she does something desperate," Mark said. "I don't know what that guilt will make her do, but it won't be good."

As we prepared to search for Maria, I couldn't help thinking about how much easier this would be if Mark could just ask people directly whether they were killers and rely on their answers. His power didn't work that way. Sure, he could tell me someone was lying, but not why.

37

As we stood in the hotel lobby trying to figure out where Maria might have gone, Destroyer broke his silence. "The Maria witch fled her quarters while you spoke to Helena," he announced.

"Which direction did she go?" I asked.

"Into the forest, following the path toward the memorial site. However, she then deviated from the established route and headed deeper into the wilderness." I could almost see him puff out his chest in pride that his spies had found her. "I have already dispatched advance scouts to establish a perimeter and maintain visual contact."

I reported what he said, and we headed toward the burial site. Today, the trees didn't calm me. They blocked the light and seemed to loom over us, waiting to block our way.

"Your familiar has been watching us?" Helena asked. "The council, I mean."

"He is part of my team," I said. "Yes. He's kept an eye on the surrounding area. Talked the local animals into helping us."

"Will someone lead us to her?" Mark asked.

"Stupid question! I have mobilized the rural division of my expanding empire. You will be met at the burial site and escorted."

I laughed and passed it on to the others. "We'll get updates, but she's not far."

As we made our way through the forest, I reached out to various animals along the path. A family of raccoons reported that Maria had passed through their territory about twenty minutes earlier, heading toward the water. A deer mentioned that she'd been talking to herself and seemed very upset about something. No reports of her getting ready to hurt someone or herself.

"This is remarkable," Helena said quietly as she watched me communicate with a squirrel about Maria's exact location. "I had no idea protector abilities included such extensive animal communication. But then you all have different powers, right?"

"It's one of my three powers," I explained. "Though I never expected to use it for tracking suspects through the wilderness."

"Your teamwork is impressive too," Helena observed, watching Mark and D coordinate their approach based on the animal intelligence I was passing on. "We haven't had much experience with a protector, but Mrs. Vestum worked alone."

"I'm just trying different things," I said, not adding that I didn't know what I was doing really, or that I was terrified of working alone.

A jay started yelling at me. "Go to the lake. Witch on log. Short distance even for no-wing people. Talking at raccoons."

I reported and pointed down a side path. I tapped Helena's arm. "Can Maria talk to animals?"

"We all can, whether they understand or not is unclear." She frowned. "Oh, you mean is it one of her powers? No."

"The raccoons have been ordered to watch Maria," Destroyer said. "I am assessing their performance. She is attempting to find someone to help her escape. They do not listen."

Something about that left me feeling like they did understand language, not like my power that just translated any language so I could understand it. I suppose knowing some basic words was a survival mechanism. "We're almost there."

As we got closer, I could hear Maria's voice through the trees. She sounded frustrated and increasingly desperate. "Please," she was saying to what I assumed were the raccoons. "I just need you to watch for people coming this way. I'm not asking you to do anything dangerous."

"It sounds like she wants a warning," Helena said quietly. "I have no guess why."

"That might make her more dangerous, not less," Mark pointed out. "People do unpredictable things when they're cornered."

"Maybe she's hoping we'll give up and leave," I said, catching myself as I tripped on a loose pebble. "But she can't stay out here indefinitely, especially without supplies. And what will time help her do?"

"We could get behind her," Mark said. "Me and D. Just to cut off her escape routes."

"Good idea, but don't hide," I said. "If she sees she's surrounded but we're not being aggressive, she might be more willing to cooperate."

38

W hen we approached, I was shocked by the change in Maria. Her silver hair was disheveled, and her usually immaculate appearance was rumpled from her flight through the forest. She didn't try to smooth her appearance when she saw us.

"I suppose it was inevitable," she said quietly. "I couldn't run far enough to escape what I've done. You would have found me no matter what."

"Maria," I said gently, settling onto the end of the log. Helena stood behind me. "We know you killed Amalia. What we want to understand is why."

She was quiet for a long moment, staring out at the dark water. Around us, I could sense various small animals watching from the underbrush—Destroyer's surveillance network maintaining their perimeter. Thankfully, Destroyer let me think without commenting.

"You wouldn't understand," Maria said finally. "You're too young, and you haven't seen what happens when communities fall apart."

"Try me," I said.

Maria turned to look at me directly, and I could see the weight of guilt and conviction warring in her expression. "Amalia was going to destroy everything we've built. Her report, her push for collaborative governance, her insistence that individual rights matter more than community security —it would have led to chaos."

"How could being a little more flexible lead to chaos?" Helena asked. She'd stepped a little closer to Maria. "She wasn't asking us to put on a show of magic and say 'tada, magic exists.'"

"Because it would have exposed how hard some of our choices have been," Maria said, her voice growing stronger as she began to justify her actions. "The tough decisions we've made to keep entire communities safe—Amalia was going to present all of that as evidence of authoritarian over-reach. We were protecting the community, not trampling people's rights."

D moved closer, joining us at the log now that it seemed she wasn't going to bolt. "But weren't some of those decisions questionable?" he asked gently.

"Of course they were questionable!" Maria snapped. "Every decision that prioritizes community welfare over individual desires is questionable. But they were necessary. And Amalia's naive idealism was going to paint them all as evidence that our councils had become too powerful."

"So you decided to stop her?" Mark said.

"I tried to reason with her first," Maria said, and I could hear the genuine pain in her voice. "For months, I tried to explain why her approach was dangerous. But she wouldn't listen. She was convinced that transparency and collaboration could solve problems that have existed for centuries."

"What happened the night she died?" I asked, getting

tired of the justification. I understood it, but I never liked the "for the common good" excuse.

Maria closed her eyes. "I went to her room to make one final attempt to convince her to abandon the documentation project. I brought tea as a peace offering—chamomile, because I knew she had trouble sleeping when she was stressed."

Not just chamomile. "And?"

"She refused to even consider dropping the project. Said she had a moral obligation to present the evidence to the other councils, even to the protectors and worldwide councils. Said that our fear of scrutiny proved that we were doing things wrong." Maria's voice broke slightly. "She was so self-righteous, so certain that her way was the only ethical path."

"So you poisoned the tea?" Mark said. "Or was it already done?"

The answer wouldn't make much difference to her punishment, but I wanted to know.

"I had prepared a sleeping draft," Maria admitted. "My plan was to make her unconscious so I could search her room and destroy the documentation. Make her start again, hoping she wouldn't. But..."

"But you gave her too much," Helena said softly, reaching for Maria's hand.

"I was angry and scared, and I miscalculated the dosage," Maria said. "By the time I realized what I'd done and gathered a healing spell, it was too late. She was gone."

The forest around us was completely quiet except for the gentle lapping of water against the shore. Even Destroyer's surveillance network seemed to be holding their breath.

"Maria," I said carefully, "you know what you did was wrong, don't you?"

"Wrong?" Maria looked at me with genuine confusion.

"Wrong to protect thousands of people from the chaos Amalia would have unleashed? Wrong to preserve the stability that keeps our communities safe?"

I realized that Maria still believed, even now, that her actions had been justified. The guilt she'd been carrying wasn't about committing murder—it was about the methods she'd been forced to use.

"You killed someone," I said firmly. "Whatever your reasons, you ended another person's life to prevent them from exercising their judgment about community governance."

"I stopped someone from destroying everything I've spent my life building," Maria replied, but her voice lacked conviction. "I was part of councils all over this continent. I saw all the bad outcomes from being soft."

"I can't believe this is the whole truth," Helena said. "There must be something worse. Other councils are not so rigid, so this must be the first time she's tried to enforce rules."

Maria slumped forward, the fight going out of her as she realized the hopelessness of her situation.

"I could force you to tell us the complete truth," I said quietly. "My protector power would compel you to answer any question I asked. But I don't want to do that unless I have to."

"Why not?" Maria asked, looking genuinely curious. "It's what I would do."

"Because I'm hoping that you can choose to tell us what really happened. That you can recognize that what you did was wrong and work with us to find a way forward that doesn't just involve punishment."

Maria stared at me for a long moment. "Do you really believe that people can be rehabilitated rather than just

imprisoned? That's surprising and, quite frankly, frighten-
ingly naive in a protector."

"I believe that people who commit crimes out of
misguided conviction might be different from people who
commit crimes out of selfishness or cruelty," I said. "But first,
you have to acknowledge that what you did was wrong,
regardless of your reasons."

39

"We're not going back to the hotel until we understand the whole truth," I said, settling more comfortably on my rock. "Out here, we can use magic freely without worrying about mundane observers. And Maria, you need to decide whether you're going to tell us everything willingly, or whether I'll have to compel the answers from you."

Maria looked around at our small group—me, Mark, D, and Helena—all waiting patiently by the moonlit lake. Destroyer would tell me if anyone approached who shouldn't learn what we talked about, or see magic if it came to that.

"Why don't I tell you what we know already to start you off," Mark said, pulling out his notebook. He gave a quick update of all the information we'd received from our interviews and the animals. "Maria, now why don't you walk us through the entire evening of Amalia's death, from dinner onward. This time don't leave out anything."

Maria sighed deeply. "After dinner, we went to the conference room for our discussion. You know about the argument—I've already admitted that Amalia and I disagreed about community management approaches."

That one word, management, was the root of the problem. My research told me that councils led communities. Management was likely where Maria got the idea they could rule.

"What specifically triggered the escalation that night?" Mark pressed. I let him continue because it gave me the space to think through the implications, not just hear the words. Was I actually figuring out my role?

"She announced that she planned to present her findings and recommendations at the next regional council meeting—you may not know, but five of the local councils meet twice a year to share news. Amalia told me her work wasn't just a report, but evidence that our councils needed fundamental restructuring." Maria's voice grew tight. "She had examples from twelve different communities, including detailed critiques of decisions I had personally been involved in."

"What happened after the meeting officially ended?" D asked, taking his turn to keep her from digging in too deep on rationale.

"I stayed behind with Helena to discuss damage control options. We both knew that Amalia's presentation would cause chaos across multiple communities." Maria glanced at Helena. "That's when I first had the idea that we needed to find a way to stop her."

"I had no idea," Helena said, her emotions verifying the truth of the statement. "I wish you had spoken to me about it. I could have... maybe talked you out of it."

"I was tired of negotiation," Maria said, frustration flaring so brightly I couldn't believe I was the only one to see it. "We kept hitting the same wall. Amalia wasn't interested in being flexible for all her talk of dropping our rules."

"So when did you decide on a more direct approach?" I asked gently.

Maria was quiet for a long moment, staring at the dark water. "Around eleven PM, I went to Amalia's room to make one final attempt at persuasion. I brought chamomile tea as a peace offering, thinking that if I could get her to relax, she might be more open to compromise. I had the sleeping draft in my pocket, just in case."

"How did it go wrong?" D asked.

"It never went right," Maria said bitterly. "Amalia was more agitated than I expected. She drank the tea quickly while explaining in detail how she planned to expose what she called authoritarian overreach in council decision-making. The more she talked, the angrier I became, and when I prepared the second cup..."

"You increased the dosage," Helena said softly.

"I was scared and furious," Maria said. "I kept thinking about how her presentation would destroy the careers of council members who had made difficult but necessary decisions. How it would undermine trust in magical governance just when we needed stability most."

"And then?" I prompted. This was the real truth finally.

"Then she started getting drowsy, but instead of stopping her lecture, she became more emotional. She started talking about how council members like me had forgotten that we were supposed to serve our communities, not control them." Maria's voice broke. "She said I had become the threat to our safety."

"That's when you gave her the fatal dose," Mark said.

"I prepared one more cup, telling myself it would just make her sleep deeply enough that I could complete my search without her waking up. But..." Maria closed her eyes. "But part of me knew I was giving her too much. Part of me wanted her to stop talking forever."

The forest around us was completely silent except for the gentle sounds of the lake. Even the insects were hushed.

"Maria," I said carefully, "you know what I can do as a protector. You are holding something back. It's painful, but I need to understand everything."

"Why does it matter?" Maria asked. "The result is the same either way. Prison and no power to protect the world."

"It matters because why you did it is as important as what you did when I decide on your punishment. It matters because if I have to compel you, it tells me you aren't ready to heal."

Maria looked at each of us in turn, then stared out at the lake for a long moment.

"What do you want to know?" she asked finally.

"Everything," I said. "The real reason you were so afraid of Amalia's project. Why you thought murder was preferable to letting her present her evidence. And most importantly, whether you understand that there could never be a justification for what you did."

Maria took a deep breath and began to speak.

40

Maria stared at the dark water for a long moment before she began to speak, her voice barely above a whisper.

"When I was twenty-three, I attended a protest in downtown Vancouver. It was supposed to be a peaceful demonstration about environmental protection, and I thought it would be safe to participate." She paused, wrapping her arms around herself. "I had excellent control of my powers back then—I thought I could blend in with mundane humans without any problems."

"What happened?" Helena asked gently.

"The protest turned violent. Not because of us, but because counter-protesters started throwing things. The police moved in with riot gear, and suddenly there were people running and screaming everywhere." Maria's voice became strained. "I found myself trapped against a building with nowhere to go."

"Were you arrested?" Mark asked.

"Almost. A police officer grabbed me and was about to put me in handcuffs when I panicked. The only thing I could think of was to trigger a spell. I didn't think about consequences. Suddenly, every piece of glass in the storefront behind us shattered." Maria shuddered at the memory. "The officer let go of me because he thought there was an attack. I managed to disappear into the crowd. But for those few seconds..."

"You were completely powerless," I said, understanding beginning to dawn.

"Completely at the mercy of mundane human authority," Maria confirmed. "And the terror of that moment—knowing that if they had arrested me, my magical abilities would have been exposed under stress, knowing that I could have been imprisoned or worse, exposed as a witch—that terror has shaped every decision I've made since then."

"Is that when you began to value security over everything else?" D asked.

"Every policy I've supported, every decision I've made as a council member, has been about preventing magical people from ever being vulnerable to mundane human control." Maria's voice grew stronger as she explained her motivation. "I wasn't blind to consequences. Believe me, at first I thought the best thing to do was retreat to somewhere isolated, where we could create our own Henbane."

"That's not really possible," Helena said. "We have lives, we need things we can't make or grow ourselves."

That didn't register as anything but justification in Maria's emotions. "Yes, and there isn't really a place that's truly isolated and actually habitable. So I did what I could to protect us."

"And Amalia's collaborative approach felt like a threat to that safety," Helena said.

"More than a threat—it felt like a deliberate attempt to weaken the very protections that keep us alive." Maria turned to look at me directly. "And then the situation with Marcus Reeves was the final evidence that we were at risk."

"Marcus isn't a risk," I said. "He's a child. Proper training will stabilize his power."

"He was a child whose uncontrolled magic had already drawn mundane attention, and instead of implementing proper containment protocols, Amalia wanted us to be even more lenient. She argued against the boarding school option, against relocating the family, against every sensible precaution we could have taken."

Relocating them from Thunder Bay hadn't done anything but make the problem worse. "But we found a good solution," I pointed out. "Marcus is safe and happy on Henbane."

"You found a solution that worked for one family," Maria said. "But what about the next case? And the one after that? Amalia's approach would have established precedents that made it impossible to protect communities from exposure risks."

"So you decided to kill her," Mark said bluntly.

"I decided to stop her from destroying everything I've spent my adult life building," Maria corrected. "When she announced her intention to present to the regional council, I knew she was going to undo decades of careful policy development. The other councils would have agreed with her."

"But those policies were wrong and didn't keep you safe," I said.

"Not wrong, harsh. And we didn't get to apply them— you stepped in," Maria said firmly. "Because harsh policies that keep us hidden are better than collaborative approaches that get us exposed, imprisoned, or killed by mundane humans."

"And Manning Park seemed like the perfect place to act?" D asked.

"It was isolated, away from our normal communities, with enough mundane activity to make things look normal." Maria's voice became matter-of-fact as she described her planning. "If Amalia died here of natural causes during a retreat, it would be sad but not suspicious. And her project would die with her."

"But you didn't plan for a protector to be called in," Helena pointed out. "You didn't want us to bring Cossi in."

"No," Maria admitted. "That was the one variable I didn't account for. I thought the council would treat it as a tragic but natural death and avoid drawing outside attention. When Helena and Beatrix insisted on calling Mrs. Vestum, I knew the deception wouldn't hold up under investigation. So I did what I could. Said we should call Cossi—she was inexperienced."

"Is that why you've been so cooperative with our investigation?" I asked. "Because you thought I'd give up and let you get on with life?"

"Partly," Maria said. "But also because I wanted you to understand that I wasn't a bad person. I didn't act out of malice or personal gain. Everything I did was to protect our communities from the kind of exposure that would destroy us."

"Maria," I said carefully, "do you understand that murder is wrong regardless of your motivations?" This was important. Was she like Phillip, unable to see right from wrong?

She was quiet for a long moment. "I understand that taking a life is a terrible thing," she said finally. "But I also believe that sometimes terrible things are necessary to prevent even worse outcomes."

"That's not the same as understanding that what you did was wrong," Mark pointed out.

"No," Maria agreed. "It's not. And I don't know if I'll ever be able to see it that way, because I can't forget the terror of being powerless in mundane human hands. Everything I've done since then has been about making sure that never happens to anyone in our communities."

41

"**D**," I said as we prepared to return to the hotel, "can you go ahead and cast a deflection spell for any plain humans we might encounter? We need to get Maria back inside without raising questions."

"Already on it," D said, pulling out a small spell bag and placing it in Maria's pocket. "Anyone who sees us will think we're just returning from a late afternoon nature walk."

The trip back through the forest was quiet, with Maria walking between Mark and me while Helena and D came behind us. Destroyer flew over us, telling us when to hide because someone was on the path ahead.

"Maria's room," I said quietly as we entered through the back entrance in the residential wing. "We need to secure her there until we can decide on next steps."

Once we had Maria settled in her room, Mark cast a containment spell that would prevent her from leaving but wouldn't cause her physical discomfort.

"I'm not trying to escape," Maria said as she sat heavily in the chair by the window. "There's nowhere to go, and when the world goes mad, you will know I'm right."

"We'll be back in to discuss arrangements," I told her. "Try to get some rest while we talk to the council."

An hour later, the remaining Vancouver council members—Elizabeth, Robert, James, Ormand, Helena, and Beatrix—gathered in the conference room for what I knew would be a difficult conversation.

"Maria has confessed to murdering Amalia Svoboda," I began without preamble. "The question now is how to handle her punishment in a way that serves justice while also addressing the underlying issues that led to this tragedy."

"What kind of underlying issues?" Elizabeth asked. "How has she justified her actions?"

I explained Maria's history and the trauma that had driven her extreme fear of exposure to mundane authority. "She genuinely believed that killing Amalia was necessary to protect magical communities from chaos and exposure."

"That doesn't excuse murder," Ormand said firmly. "There were many ways to resolve this disagreement. If she had only told us about the protest..."

"Maria made up her mind," I said, even though I agreed with him. "But it does suggest that simple punishment might not be sufficient. Maria needs help dealing with her trauma, or she'll never understand why her actions were wrong."

"What are you proposing?" Beatrix asked. "We have our own rules, but given that they were mostly created by a murderer, we cannot rely on their fairness."

"As far as I know, the sentence for murder is life imprisonment in the local facility," I said. "But I'd like to suggest a modified approach."

"Modified how?" Helena asked. "You pushed Maria to tell us about her past for a reason. Now we need to know."

"Maria goes to the prison as required, but with the possibility of eventual rehabilitation if she can work through her trauma and genuinely understand why murder was wrong, regardless of her motivations. It will be a better outcome than her stewing in fear for the rest of her life."

Robert looked skeptical. "Has that kind of rehabilitation ever worked before? And what if she heals herself?"

"I don't know," I admitted. "But I think it's worth trying, especially since Maria's crime was driven by ideology rather than personal malice. I'm not proposing that she be released, just healed."

"This sounds like something the plain humans attempt. What would rehabilitation look like?" James asked.

"Therapy to address her trauma about mundane authority. Education about alternative approaches to community protection. And most importantly, genuine acknowledgment that her actions were wrong, not just regrettable. I think her sentence will be easier on her if she is able to let go of the fear."

Elizabeth was quiet for a moment. "If Maria is held in prison while it happens, I don't see the danger." She looked at her fellow council members. "Does anyone object?"

I didn't think their objections would matter. Not to be braggy, but I am a protector and my word goes. At least that's what I'm doing my best to believe. "There's something else. This situation could have been avoided if you'd called for help earlier instead of trying to handle everything internally."

"What do you mean?" Helena asked, her emotions spilling over now that the situation no longer weighed on her. Bright pink relief, shot through with threads of purple surprise.

"According to Mrs. V, many community problems can be

resolved with a simple phone call or video conference. You don't need to wait until there's a crisis to reach out for guidance." I looked around the table. "If Maria had been able to discuss her fears about Amalia's project with an outside authority before those fears drove her to desperate measures, Amalia might still be alive."

"You're suggesting we should have called a protector about philosophical disagreements?" Ormand asked.

"I'm suggesting you should have called for guidance when those philosophical disagreements started affecting the way you protect the community," I said. "Prevention is much easier than crisis management."

"That's... actually a very good point," Beatrix said thoughtfully. "We've been so focused on maintaining independence that we've avoided seeking help until situations become unmanageable. I may not have fully agreed with Amalia, but she did have a lot of good points."

As the meeting concluded and council members dispersed to their rooms, I didn't want to be alone. We went to the small bar in the lobby to talk. Destroyer returned to his imperial plans, so I didn't have a peanut gallery to deal with.

"How do you feel about the resolution?" Mark asked. "Will it change anything?"

I thought about the question for a moment. Did I feel anything but relief? Yes, definitely. "I learned that my job isn't really about solving crimes or preventing magical exposure. There are more threats to the magical communities than that, both internal and external. We need to figure out how differently each council works. We protectors need to stop being alone."

42

The next morning brought clear skies and a snap of the cold weather to come, along with the crisp mountain air. Since we had to wait for the guards to arrive to transport Maria, we decided to make the most of our unexpected free day.

"Picnic by the lake?" D suggested as we finished breakfast. "After everything that's happened, I think we could all use some time to decompress."

"Good idea," I said, thinking how easy it was to hang out with both of the men who'd found a way into my heart. One day I'd have to choose, but not today. "I'm pretty sure this won't be the last crisis I have to solve, so I'll take the breaks where they come."

The hotel kitchen was happy to pack us a lunch, and soon we were settled on a blanket beside the same lake where we'd found Maria the night before. In daylight, it was peaceful and beautiful, with no trace of the drama that had unfolded there.

"So," Mark said, unwrapping a sandwich, "you've had a

night to think about it. What did you learn from being
here?"

"That it's a lot more complicated than I expected," I said
honestly. "On Henbane, everyone wants to help solve problems—well, except the witch who created them. Here,
people had their own agendas and weren't always honest
about what they knew."

"None of us are prepared for this kind of thing," Mark
said. "Communities that live among mundane humans
develop different survival strategies, I get that, but I don't see
how they got to such extremes."

"I had a hard time using anything but my protector
power," I said, picking at the food on my lap. "I could barely
read the emotions, and the animals were all over the place,
but only a few were willing to help."

"You adapted well, though," D said. "You found the truth.
Destroyer was helpful without taking over the world. And
maybe you should look for a shield-breaker spell."

"Priorities," Destroyer said, landing on my shoulder.
"Building an empire is a long-term project. You will not
achieve unity in a day."

I passed along his comments and we all laughed. More a
release of tension than appreciating crow humor.

"I guess I'm relying too much on you all for help. I need
to be able to operate alone, right?" I crossed my fingers, if
that means anything, that I would be old and way more
experienced before that happened.

"You've done it without me," Mark said. "And you did all
the work this time. You'll be fine."

I appreciated his words, but I'd never done an investigation truly alone.

"A wise emperor prepares for all contingencies,"
Destroyer replied with dignity. "Should you require solo

operations, I shall establish communication protocols with local wildlife in advance."

I kept his promise to myself but thanked him for the comfort. Time to change the subject. I couldn't really expect them to help me with protector stuff. That was for when I got back home.

"I'm not going to worry about the possibilities. We only have a few more hours before we head out. Destroyer, make the most of your freedom."

He flapped his wings on my shoulder where he'd been staring at my sandwich and disappeared into the trees.

"I'd be interested in learning more about the world," D said. "I mean, it's one thing to be online, and a whole other thing to be in person."

"You planning to take some time off?" Mark asked. "Who will tell us to reboot our laptops or clear our cache?"

D gave him a not-so-gentle shove. "I wasn't planning on a long time away. I can train someone. And I don't know where to pick for my first adventure. Cossi, do you have any suggestions?"

I'd been lost in my thoughts and the peace of the forest, only paying casual attention to their conversations. "Probably the usual, Paris, Hawaii, Vietnam. I'm just happy to live a quiet life on Henbane for the next couple of centuries."

We spent the rest of the afternoon talking about everything but the case. We finished eating and took a hike around a short trail. I chatted with a few squirrels. We saw something large in the distance—a moose, or an elk, or something. It didn't respond to my call, just stood there staring at us. My worries about the future fell to the bottom of my thoughts, kind of like sediment in a river. Okay, I need better metaphors.

When we returned to the lodge, a pair of black SUVs

lurked in the parking lot. Vehicle of choice for intimidation of criminals—and me.

"So, we can go home," Mark said, waving to the two witches standing at the entrance to the lodge.

"I'm looking forward to that," I said. "Though I'm pretty sure Mrs. V won't let me relax for too long."

Mark left us to help the guards. D and I wandered through the lobby of the hotel to collect our bags. Destroyer's cage was still in our vehicle. We'd checked out before heading to our picnic so there would be no delays on the way home.

"She'll always have something to teach you," he said. "Not every protector job is exciting."

"You'd be surprised how stimulating practicing ancient spells can be," I said. "Especially when one of them turns on you and you find yourself covered in foul-smelling slime."

43

The next morning brought clear skies and a snap of the cold weather to come, along with the crisp mountain air. Since we had to wait for the guards to arrive to transport Maria, we decided to make the most of our unexpected free day.

"Picnic by the lake?" D suggested as we finished breakfast. "After everything that's happened, I think we could all use some time to decompress."

"Good idea," I said, thinking how easy it was to hang out with both of the men who'd found a way into my heart. One day I'd have to choose, but not today. "I'm pretty sure this won't be the last crisis I have to solve, so I'll take the breaks where they come."

The hotel kitchen was happy to pack us a lunch, and soon we were settled on a blanket beside the same lake where we'd found Maria the night before. In daylight, it was peaceful and beautiful, with no trace of the drama that had unfolded there.

"So," Mark said, unwrapping a sandwich, "you've had a

night to think about it. What did you learn from being here?"

"That it's a lot more complicated than I expected," I said honestly. "On Henbane, everyone wants to help solve problems—well, except the witch who created them. Here, people had their own agendas and weren't always honest about what they knew."

"None of us are prepared for this kind of thing," Mark said. "Communities that live among mundane humans develop different survival strategies, I get that, but I don't see how they got to such extremes."

"I had a hard time using anything but my protector power," I said, picking at the food on my lap. "I could barely read the emotions, and the animals were all over the place, but only a few were willing to help."

"You adapted well, though," D said. "You found the truth. Destroyer was helpful without taking over the world. And maybe you should look for a shield-breaker spell."

"Priorities," Destroyer said, landing on my shoulder. "Building an empire is a long-term project. You will not achieve unity in a day."

I passed along his comments and we all laughed. More a release of tension than appreciating crow humor.

"I guess I'm relying too much on you all for help. I need to be able to operate alone, right?" I crossed my fingers, if that means anything, that I would be old and way more experienced before that happened.

"You've done it without me," Mark said. "And you did all the work this time. You'll be fine."

I appreciated his words, but I'd never done an investigation truly alone.

"A wise emperor prepares for all contingencies," Destroyer replied with dignity. "Should you require solo operations, I shall establish communication protocols with local wildlife in advance."

I kept his promise to myself but thanked him for the comfort. Time to change the subject. I couldn't really expect them to help me with protector stuff. That was for when I got back home.

"I'm not going to worry about the possibilities. We only have a few more hours before we head out. Destroyer, make the most of your freedom."

He flapped his wings on my shoulder where he'd been staring at my sandwich and disappeared into the trees.

"I'd be interested in learning more about the world," D said. "I mean, it's one thing to be online, and a whole other thing to be in person."

"You planning to take some time off?" Mark asked. "Who will tell us to reboot our laptops or clear our cache?"

D gave him a not-so-gentle shove. "I wasn't planning on a long time away. I can train someone. And I don't know where to pick for my first adventure. Cossi, do you have any suggestions?"

I'd been lost in my thoughts and the peace of the forest, only paying casual attention to their conversations. "Probably the usual—Paris, Hawaii, Vietnam. I'm just happy to live a quiet life on Henbane for the next couple of centuries."

We spent the rest of the afternoon talking about everything but the case. We finished eating and took a hike around a short trail. I chatted with a few squirrels. We saw something large in the distance—a moose, or an elk, or something. It didn't respond to my call, just stood there staring at us. My worries about the future fell to the bottom of my thoughts, kind of like sediment in a river. Okay, I need better metaphors.

When we returned to the lodge, a pair of black SUVs lurked in the parking lot. Vehicle of choice for intimidation of criminals—and me.

"So, we can go home," Mark said, waving to the two witches standing at the entrance to the lodge.

"I'm looking forward to that," I said. "Though I'm pretty sure Mrs. V won't let me relax for too long."

Mark left us to help the guards. D and I wandered through the lobby of the hotel to collect our bags. Destroyer's cage was still in our vehicle. We'd checked out before heading to our picnic so there would be no delays on the way home.

"She'll always have something to teach you," he said. "Not every protector job is exciting."

"You'd be surprised how stimulating practicing ancient spells can be," I said. "Especially when one of them turns on you and you find yourself covered in foul-smelling slime."

WANT MORE

Cossi's biggest fear comes true on her favorite holiday. German Christmas markets and dead bodies. Are horrible, but this time Cossi is solving the case alone.

Use the QR code to check out A Strange Spell

If you enjoyed reading Murder Magic and Mayhem please

consider helping other readers to find the story by using the QR code to leave a review.

FREE BOOK

Claim your copy of Magic Will Out when you sign up for my newsletter and follow Cossi as she seeks answers to her past.

ALSO BY POPPY

For more books by Poppy Bridgeman
scan the QR code below.

ABOUT POPPY BRIDGEMAN

Hi, I'm Poppy Bridgeman, the cozy mystery alter ego of Canadian author P A Wilson. Poppy was "born" because sometimes stories need a gentler touch—with a little magic, a dash of humor, and plenty of sleuthing spirit.

As Poppy, I write the *Witch of Henbane Island* series (where witches and festivals collide with mysteries), the *EB Eats Culinary Mysteries* (a small-town diner, a determined heroine, and murder on the menu), and the *Pages & Paws Bookstore Mysteries* (a Devon bookshop, two mischievous corgis, and plenty of secrets tucked between the shelves).

When I'm not tangled in my characters' escapades, I'm happily tangled in yarn—I knit, weave, and doodle in sketchbooks between writing sessions. I also love to travel, finding inspiration for charming settings, quirky characters, and suspicious strangers wherever I go.

Home base is the Vancouver area, where I juggle writing as both Poppy and P A Wilson. Whichever name is on the cover, I'm always chasing the next story.

ACKNOWLEDGMENTS

People think that the process of writing is solitary. That's not the case for me. I have help from so many people it would be hard to acknowledge everyone, but I'll give it a try.

The support and inspiration I get from my writer's groups is incalculable. The Vancouver Writers Social Group opens my mind to other ways of telling a story. The Royal City Literary Arts Society gives me the opportunity to meet and share with other writers who have more knowledge than I do. The Other 11 Months group is where I learn about getting the words on the page. And my critique group who helps me find the best parts of the story I want to tell. Thanks to all of the members of these great groups.

Last of all, but definitely a huge part of the process, my beta readers. These are the people who love stories and are willing, and more than able, to tell me if my finished story is ready for you, my readers.

www.ingramcontent.com/pod-product-compliance
Lightning Source LLC
Chambersburg PA
CBHW020611180626
46810CB00007B/2728